# Ghost
## of a
# Chance

### By
# Flip Kobler & Cindy Marcus

A Samuel French Acting Edition

# SAMUEL FRENCH
FOUNDED 1830

New York  Hollywood  London  Toronto

SAMUELFRENCH.COM

ISBN   978-0-573-62710-1      Printed   in   U.S.A.      #9909

## IMPORTANT BILLING AND CREDIT
## REQUIREMENTS

All producers of GHOST OF A CHANCE *must* give credit to the Authors of the Play in all programs distributed in connection with performances of the Play and in all instances in which the title of the Play appears for purposes of advertising, publicizing or otherwise exploiting the Play and/or a production. The names of the Authors *must* also appear on a separate line, on which no other name appears, immediately following the title, and *must* appear in size of type not less than fifty percent the size of the title type.

GHOST OF A CHANCE was first presented at the Francis Wilson Playhouse in Clearwater, Fla. on June 15th, 1995. Set design was by Fred Kobler. Lighting and sound design was by Richard Traylor. The lighting and sound technician was Ric Dorrie. The stage manager was Graham Artingstoll. The costumes were designed by Joan McCool. Jeff Fullerton was the assistant director and the production was directed by Cindy Marcus.

| | |
|---|---|
| FLOYD | Jim Ulmer |
| VERNA | Ginger King |
| BETHANY | Jessica Matthews |
| CHANCE | Flip Kobler |
| CRYSTAL | Greta Beckett |
| ADAM LUCAS | Fred Kobler |

GHOST OF A CHANCE was presented on January 11, 1997 at the West Valley JCC in Los Angeles. Set design was by Fred Kobler. The lighting director was Irwin Mechanic. Sound design was by Larry Pierce. The stage manager was Ray Sternberg. Costumes were designed by Ann Mashiyama. The production was directed by Cindy Marcus.

| | |
|---|---|
| FLOYD | Jim Ulmer |
| VERNA | Ruth Marcus |
| BETHANY | Peggy O'Neal |
| CHANCE | Flip Kobler |
| CRYSTAL | Knekoh Fruge |
| ADAM LUCAS | Brad Green |

# CHARACTERS

BETHANY: A new woman. Bright, strong, independent, beautiful. But she's a locked vault, living life only for tomorrow. Unwilling to face her past; when it comes back to haunt her, she is unprepared to deal with it. An emotional roller-coaster that reverts her to the woman she was. Dependency - 10, self esteem - 0.

FLOYD: Beth's fiancée. The tortoise. Stable. Safe. Durable. Excitement and adventure are things he's read about in books. But he loves Bethany, and when that is threatened he is going to break out of his shell. Even if it kills him.

CHANCE: Beth's first husband. The hare. Wild and free. Living fast and hard. Adventure was his middle name. He loves Beth as well and he's not about to let a little thing like his own death keep him from spending the rest of their life together. Not at any cost. Any.

VERNA: Floyd's mother. Protective and suspicious. Looking at life in a rose-colored rear-view mirror. She's convinced herself that her dislike of Beth is all for her son's own good, not because she sees herself in Beth's eyes.

CRYSTAL: Flamboyant with a capitol FLAM. Actually with a capitol BOYANT as well. Cigar-chomping, vodka-swilling kook, squeezing the life out of each and every moment. A psychic with a sarcastic edge that's Wilkenson sharp. But there's a darkness behind that party girl façade.

ADAM: Verna's age. A Kris Kringle face, happy-go-lucky charm that's contagious. But he's seen his one chance for an Easy Street address and is going to take it. Grandpa Walton turned reluctant Dillinger.

## THE PLACE
A cabin in Connecticut

## THE TIME

ACT I
Scene 1 - Late Friday night
Scene 2 - Noon Saturday
Scene 3 - Saturday at sunset

ACT II
Scene 1 - A few moments later
Scene 2 - *Early* Sunday morning
Scene 3 - Later Sunday
Scene 4 - Monday morning

*For our parents;*
*Fred & Dorothy Kobler*
*and*
*Ruth & Sy Marcus,*

*Who taught us to taste Wind and Rain*

## ACT I
### Scene 1

*(We're in a cabin. Au de testosterone. A couple of deer heads mounted here and there. A rock fireplace on the stage right wall. An entrance to the kitchen just north of that. Smack in the middle of the back wall is a manly mahogany door. Windows in the back wall will look out over a forest, lots of green and smelling like Pine-Sol. Steps leading upstairs grace the stage left wall. A closer door is just downstage of them. There's a leather sofa, a brawny coffee table and dark Lazy Boy sitting on a virile throw rug.*

*That's all fine and dandy, but as the curtain rises we can't see squat. The place is dark. No lights. We do however get a sense that something is lying smack in the middle of the rug. Crickets chirp and we hear a CAR PULL UP. Flashlights swish through the dark trees outside, like Jedi Light-sabers. After a few moments we can hear KEYS JIGGLING outside and soon enough the door opens, HINGES SQUEAKING. It's been a while since it's been used.)*

FLOYD. Here we go. *(FLOYD scratches at the wall until he finds the light switch. The room erupts in all its robust glory. And yup, we were right. There was something on the floor. A BODY! It just lays there, dead as a door nail. It's currently hidden by the sofa, and nobody upstage will see it for a while. FLOYD enters, carrying several suitcases and sets them down, surveying the place. VERNA enters behind him, letting her eyes wander the room.)* Wow, this isn't so bad. Is it? Do you think it is Mother?

*(VERNA shrugs and grunts once.)*

FLOYD. Yeah, you're probably right. But the way Bethany ran it down I was expecting a little shack. This is kinda nice. Huh? Up here in the mountains. Huh? Lots of trees. "One touch of nature makes the whole world kin." Shakespeare.

VERNA. One touch of nature will give you a nasty rash. Did you bring my —

FLOYD. Ointment. In the suitcase.

VERNA. And your —

FLOYD. Asthma medicine. Right here.

*(VERNA takes a tour around the place, always just out of eyeshot of the body.)*

VERNA: So, whose place is this again?

FLOYD. *His.*

VERNA. Ah yes, the Great White Hunter. *(She stops in front of the fireplace, staring up into the deer's head mounted there. It gives her the willies and she starts to back up ... and up ... and ... just a few inches from stepping on the body now ...)* How long are we staying?

FLOYD. Just long enough to get the house in order. Pack up the personal belongings. The new owner is coming by first thing Monday morning.

VERNA. Good. I don't know if I could stay long, with this poor little guy staring at me with those sad eyes. Look at them. Little Doe eyes.

FLOYD. They're not real. I think they're glass.

VERNA. Glass eyes?! What kind of man would hunt a blind deer?

FLOYD. The taxidermist puts them in.

VERNA. Oh. I'm surprised he didn't stuff it himself. Gut it. Skin it. Drink the blood of his victims. *(She missed the body altogether and stands, surveying the room. She and Floyd are mirror images, hands on hips, scanning left to right. Tweedle Dee and Tweedle Dum. Halves of the same whole. Verna moves to the mantel, picking up a coffee mug and looking inside.)* Ugh. Doesn't anybody clean this place?

FLOYD. She hasn't been up here in three years. Not since ...

VERNA. Yes. Fine. Whatever. Well, as long as we're here, you might as well go help your father inside.

FLOYD. Mother.

VERNA. Go on. Go on. You know how he hates to be kept waiting. *(FLOYD rolls his eyes and heads back out. VERNA takes a closer look around, snooping at this and that, but just always out of sight of that damn body. After a few moments FLOYD re-enters with another suitcase.)* Where's your father?

FLOYD. Right here.

VERNA. Well, help him in.

*(FLOYD steps out and instantly comes back. But this time he's carrying a cremation urn. He feels like a dork for schlepping it. He tries to hand it over to VERNA, but she's busy looking about.)*

FLOYD. Here.

VERNA. Show him around.

FLOYD. *(Holding the urn out at arms length and displaying it to the room.)* Here we are Dad. Here's the room. Fireplace. Kitchen. Basement. Our bedrooms are upstairs. And here's where you'll be staying. Hope you like it. *(And he sets it down on a liquor cabinet near the window. Right next to a completely dead potted plant.)* I'm going to get the rest of the things.

VERNA. One at a time, dear. What would I do if you put your back out. What have I always told you? Better —

VERNA and FLOYD. — safe than sorry.

*(He vanishes. VERNA opens the drapes and turns the urn to a better view.)*

VERNA. This is perfect, where you can see the forest. Can you smell the pine? Careful of your allergies, this isn't like the park. How long have we been going to that park on Broad Street? Forty ... forty-two years. Twice a week for forty-two years. Now that's love. In our day people took their time about things. Not running off, getting engaged after barely a year.

*(VERNA checks to see if she's alone, then systematically starts*

*searching the room as she talks. But she always manages to
somehow turn at the last moment, or keep her back to that
body ...)*

VERNA. Oh Harold, what are we going to do? *Your* son is
determined to marry this girl. And we don't know anything about
her. *(She takes a few steps backwards, nearly tripping over the
feet of the body ... but she stops half an inch short and starts forward again ...)* She refuses to talk about her past. It's like she just
came out of the womb at thirty years old. My God, can you imagine her mother's labor. I thought Floyd was a big baby. She's
hiding something. *(She's behind the sofa now, hands resting on
the back of it. If she'd just look down she'd see it. But she stares
at the ceiling in thought ...)* I can sense it. It's something
small ... *(A noise behind her and —)* Bethany? *(Nope, just
Floyd.)* Oh, I thought you were Bethany.
FLOYD. No, her hair is longer.
VERNA. Where is she?
FLOYD. She walked down to get the mail.
VERNA. Where? In Miami? How long can that take?
FLOYD. The mail box is nearly a mile away. We didn't drive by
it because that mountain road looked a little dangerous.
VERNA. How quaint. Where's the telephone? Down by Goo-
ber's general store? They have a bathroom around here that doesn't
require crossing a traffic light or bringing your own shovel?
FLOYD. It's hard for Bethany to face this. I feel honored that
she asked me to face this with her. How about you, huh?
VERNA. Honored? Oh yes, I feel quite honored that she
"allowed" me to still spend time with my own son before she steals
him away.
FLOYD. This is not a competition. I still love you. I'm gonna go
get the rest of the stuff.

*(He heads out. VERNA searches a little more, before she realizes —)*

VERNA. Maybe upstairs. *(So she totters up there and we're left
with a dead stage for a moment. Nothing happens. Beat. Then sud-*

*denly —)* **ARRRRRRRRGGGGHHHHHHH!!!!**

*(The body lurches up, screaming his damn head off. The howl continues until his lungs drain and the bellow slowly dies. CHANCE sits for a moment trying like hell to get his bearings, gulping air. After a moment, he recognizes the place ...)*

CHANCE. What the hell? How did I get here? Why are all the lights on? Why am I talking to myself? *(Suddenly his face gets worried. Terrified, he looks inside his shirt at his belly and sighs heavily.)* Thank God. It was all a dream. *(He crosses to the window and looks out.)* Where's my truck? Whose car is that in the driveway? *(He goes for the doorknob, but it won't budge. Not even a jiggle.)* How the hell did I get locked in? Where's my key? *(He starts looking, then the knob starts to turn. Oh, man. Panicked, he jumps over the sofa and ducks low, just as FLOYD comes back in with another load of bags.)* Burglar. Oh man, I'm being robbed. By a man who brought his own luggage. What's, he plannin' on spendin' the night? See, that's the problem with being self-employed. People got no motivation for deadlines. *(FLOYD heads upstairs and is gone. CHANCE runs to the phone on the wall.)* Cops. I'm calling the cops you putz. *(And he reaches for the phone and tugs. But the receiver won't lift. Won't budge.)* Who glued my phone? That was an expensive phone. Alright. I'll use the one in the kitchen. I have got to stop narrating my own life. *(And he's in the kitchen as FLOYD comes back down and heads out the front door. A few seconds later CHANCE comes back in.)* That must be the greatest glue in the world. If they had Olympics for glue, that's the gold medalist. So, I'm on my own. Alright pal, there's no way I'm gonna let you beat me. Let's go, tough guy!

*(And he heads upstairs, just aching for a fight. After a few moments we hear voices outside the front door.)*

BETHANY. Floyd, put me down.
FLOYD. No it's okay, I gotcha. *(He staggers in, trying to carry her over the threshold.)* This will be romantic.

BETHANY. I don't want to be romantic here. Put me down. *(He does.)* Thank you. You shouldn't do that for another two weeks anyway.

*(She turns and faces the room. The sight of it hits hard. But she sucks in a deep breath, counts to ten and is ready to face it head on. This is a strong woman.)*

FLOYD. You okay?

BETHANY. Yes. This isn't so bad. I'm strong. I'm in control of my own life. I can handle this. *(She takes a few hesitant steps into the room, testing the waters. She can handle it.)* Okay. We'll just pack up the last of the things, turn over the keys and get on with our life together. No looking back. Ever.

FLOYD. Right.

BETHANY. It will be a glorious life, won't it.

FLOYD. Anyway you want it.

BETHANY. Always wondered what this place looked like.

FLOYD. You've never been up here?

BETHANY. Oh no. This was Chance's private hideaway. Kind of a *man* thing. *(Scans the room. Notices the coffee cup on the mantle and moves toward it.)* Look at this. He left his coffee cups lying around. This must be from the day he — *(Suddenly frightened she wheels on FLOYD.)* Tell me about our life. Quickly, tell me how great it's going to be.

FLOYD. Our life will be great.

BETHANY. We'll have a house.

FLOYD. Yes. A big house. Four bedrooms.

BETHANY. Five.

FLOYD. Alright. And a two car garage. Huh?

BETHANY. And we'll have two cars. But one will be a van.

FLOYD. If you want, sure. A red van.

BETHANY. Blue.

FLOYD. Blue. With dual airbags.

BETHANY. And we'll have kids. I can get a job if I want. Go back to school if I want.

FLOYD. We'll set up a studio for your paintings. Huh? Whatever you want. As Thomas Jefferson said, "I like the dreams of the future better than the history of the past."

BETHANY. Me too. As long as I keep thinking about us, about our future I can make it through this weekend. Alright, onward and upward.

*(She heads into the kitchen. FLOYD is about to follow when —)*

CHANCE. FREEZE! *(Floyd does.)* Wait a second. Do I know you? I do, don't I! *(FLOYD doesn't move, doesn't peep. Just stands there like a contorted scarecrow. CHANCE moves towards the kitchen to get a better look at the man's face ...)* I know that face. Who are you? Answer me, pal.

*(FLOYD just wheezes, gasping for air. He pulls an asthma inhaler out of his pocket and sucks hard. He can breathe again.)*

BETHANY. Are you alright —
FLOYD. Yeah. Just a little asthma attack. I'm fine.

*(She freezes, just inches from CHANCE's face. There is a moment of shock, then —)*

CHANCE. Bethany?
BETHANY. AHHHHHHHHHHHHHHHH!
CHANCE. AHHHHHHHHHHHHHHHH!
BETHANY and CHANCE. AHHHHHHHHHHH!
BETHANY, CHANCE and FLOYD. AHHHHHHHHHHH!
CHANCE. What?
FLOYD. What is it?
CHANCE. What?
BETHANY. *(Pointing.)* It's him!
FLOYD. Who?
CHANCE. He's a burglar, Annie. Run!
BETHANY. Not him.
FLOYD. Not him who?
BETHANY. (To CHANCE:) You!

CHANCE and FLOYD. Me?
BETHANY. Not you. *Him!*
FLOYD. There's somebody else here?
CHANCE. Where?
BETHANY. Right there! Right there!
FLOYD. Right there what?
BETHANY. My husband!
FLOYD. Chance?
CHANCE. What?
BETHANY. Oh my ... god ...

*(And her eyes roll up into her head. She starts to fall but good ol' CHANCE is there to save her. But somehow she slips right through his grasp as if he weren't even there. THUNK! Sack o' potatoes into the floor. FLOYD is right there, doting over BETHANY. CHANCE stands there dazed. Just staring at his hands like he's got a hole in his racquet.)*

FLOYD. Mother!
VERNA. *(Rushing in.)* What is it? What was all the screaming? Oh my god.
FLOYD. She —
VERNA. — fainted.
CHANCE. No kidding.
FLOYD. Help me get her to the couch. *(They do.)* Bethany. Bethany. Are you alright. Can you hear me?
VERNA. I'll call a doctor.
CHANCE. You can't. Somebody glued the phone —
VERNA. *(Lifting the receiver.)* What's the number?
CHANCE. Hey.
FLOYD. It's okay. I think she's starting to come around. *(VERNA hangs up and heads back. CHANCE moves to the phone and tries to lift the receiver. No go. Can't get it to budge.)* Bethany. Are you alright?
BETHANY. I think so. I think.
CHANCE. Alright. What's the gag?
BETHANY. What happened.

FLOYD. You fainted.

BETHANY. I fainted?

VERNA. You were screaming.

BETHANY. Screaming? No. You must be mistaken. I never scream.

CHANCE. How come *I* can't get the phone up?

BETHANY. *(Seeing him again.)* AHHHHHHHHHH!

CHANCE. Will you stop that. You're giving me the willies.

BETHANY. It's him.

FLOYD. Him who?

BETHANY. Chance.

VERNA. Uh-oh.

FLOYD. You see Chance?

BETHANY. Yes.

FLOYD. Right here?

BETHANY. Yes.

FLOYD. Right now?

BETHANY. Yes.

VERNA. Uh-oh.

FLOYD. Where?

CHANCE. Right here genius. *(Off FLOYD's glasses.)* You might want to get that prescription checked.

BETHANY. *(Jamming her fists into her eyes, covering them.)* I am fine. I am strong. Go away.

VERNA. Uh-oh. I thought you said her husband was dead.

FLOYD. He is.

CHANCE. Excuse me?

BETHANY. I'm fine.

VERNA. Thought you said he died three years ago.

FLOYD. He did.

CHANCE. Excuse me?

BETHANY. I'm strong.

CHANCE. Whoa. Hello. Reality check. I am not dead.

FLOYD. Died right in this room. Right here on this floor.

*(He points right where CHANCE is standing. Right where his body was laying. Yipes! CHANCE jumps as if the spot were ablaze.)*

CHANCE. Hey. *I am not dead.* Hello?!

*(But VERNA and FLOYD ignore him. Look right at him. Through him. As if he were ... a ghost.)*

FLOYD. Do you remember? You saw him buried.
BETHANY. I don't want to remember that.
CHANCE. Hold it right there.
FLOYD. Death is a hard thing to face. But if you can admit it ... I'll tell you what. Close your eyes.
BETHANY. Floyd, I ...
FLOYD. We'll face it together.
BETHANY. We will? You and I?
CHANCE. I am not dead!
FLOYD. You and I. Now say it. Come on.
CHANCE. I am not ... *(Waving a hand frantically in front of VERNA's eyes. She doesn't even notice.)* I am not ... Oh my god. I am. I'm ...
FLOYD. Say it.
CHANCE and BETHANY. ... dead.

*(And it's his turn to faint. PLOP! Right behind the sofa. Out of sight, out of mind. BETHANY is starting to wig out. Panic attack. FLOYD is right there to coach her down. Holding her hands, a calming influence.)*

FLOYD. It's alright. You can face this. Huh? I believe in you. Breathe. Come on Bethany, we'll do it together. Breathe. Now think of our life together. The house and van. Your paintings and school. Waking up every morning together, for the rest of our lives.
VERNA. Uhn-uh!
FLOYD. I love you Bethany. *(That does it. BETHANY calms. FLOYD gently kisses her nose.)* Good job.
BETHANY. God you're sweet. I don't deserve you.

*(VERNA grunts approval.)*

FLOYD. Take a look around. Do you see him?

BETHANY. *(Doing it.)* No. No. Must have just been a figment of my imagination.

FLOYD. Sure. The strain of coming here again. Your mind plays tricks on you. You want to talk about it?

BETHANY. No. I'm just so embarrassed.

FLOYD. Don't be. My mom talks to my dad all the time.

VERNA. That's different! He doesn't answer me. I'm just carrying his memory in my heart.

FLOYD. You carry his urn in a backpack.

VERNA. Do you hear this Harold? Are you listening? *Your* son thinks I'm mentally unstable.

FLOYD. I didn't say that.

BETHANY. I am not unstable. Do you think I'm unstable —

FLOYD. Enough, okay? Please. Let's just get this done. Where are the boxes?

BETHANY. In the attic, I think.

FLOYD. No, I got it. You rest. Mother. Can you give me a hand?

VERNA. Something is wrong here. In my day, people didn't do this sort of thing.

*(And the two of them vanish upstairs. BETHANY lies there for a moment, then slowly starts to sit. Just at that same moment, CHANCE pops his head up from behind the sofa and — )*

BETHANY. AH!

CHANCE. Don't scream.

BETHANY. *(Covering her eyes.)* It's not real. It's all in your mind. Because you're thinking about the past. Don't. Think about the future.

*(She opens her eyes.)*

CHANCE. Hi.

BETHANY. *(Slamming them shut again.)* We'll have a five bedroom house and a two car garage.

*(She opens her eyes.)*

CHANCE. We need to talk.

BETHANY. *(Slamming them shut!)* I'LL GO BACK TO SCHOOL. I WILL BE HAPPY.

CHANCE. Oh stop it. *(She does.)* Look at me. *(She does.)* How many fingers am I holding up?

BETHANY. Three.

CHANCE. Good. That's good. That's great. That's apple pie ala mode. That's Christmas in Connecticut. Fantastic. You can hear me, right? So I can't be dead. You can see me, you can hear me. Look at this, I can walk on the floor. *(He jumps up and down.)* I can sit on the furniture. *(Yup, he sure can.)* I can move objects. *(He rushes to the mantel, grabs the coffee mug and turns to walk away. The mug doesn't budge. It practically rips his arm out of his socket. He tries harder. No go. Again. Nothing. Digging his heels in he leans back and with all his might now, he tries to lift the damn thing. Nada. Finally his grip slips and he crunches into the floor. He stares hard at the mug. BETHANY then walks over and gently lifts it. Proof. Beat while the weight of that sinks in.)* How can I be dead? I feel great. Great! I don't feel any pain. *(He beats himself ...)* I don't feel anything. *(Closing in on her, sniffing. She backs away ...)* Nothing. Do you still wear that sexy perfume. I can't smell. Anything. I can't feel.

BETHANY. This is all in my mind. I'll start packing.

CHANCE. God, I'm really dead. Was I buried?

BETHANY. Maybe in the kitchen.

CHANCE. Did you bury me next to my folks Annie?

BETHANY. The pots and pans first.

CHANCE. Was there a funeral? Did people come?

BETHANY. Where are those boxes?

CHANCE. Was there a viewing? What was I wearing? The navy blue pinstripe, probably. The white-on-white Armani shirt. Brocade vest. Gray striped tie ... *(She tries to break for the kitchen. He blocks her path.)* You did put me in the gray striped tie. *(She tries again.)* You didn't put me in that blue paisley thing did you? *(Her expression is enough to know she did.)* Oh, man! Annie. I hate that tie. I don't mean hate, I know you gave it to me. It's nice, it's just not right for a funeral. How many times have I told you you can't wear paisley for a formal event. If ever I should have looked my best ...

BETHANY. This is nuts. This can't be happening.

CHANCE. How do you think I feel? I'm gonna be stuck for eternity in blue paisley. I hope the pearly gates don't have a dress code. Pearly gates ... If I was buried in a suit, how come I'm wearing this? I only wear this when I come to go hunting. That's right, I remember now. *(BETHANY grabs a box and starts arbitrarily slamming whatever she can into it. Making as much distracting noise as possible. Every time CHANCE gets close to a memory for her, she bangs louder.)* I came up here to go "hunting." *(Bang.)* I went down to the glade and saw this huge buck. Seven foot antler spread. *(Bang!)* But he must've saw me. *(BANG-BANG!)* I think he got me. I lost to a deer? *(She drops the box.)* I've been hunting since I was six and I was killed by Thumper.

BETHANY. He was a bunny.

CHANCE. Alright Flower.

BETHANY. Skunk.

CHANCE. Well, which was the deer?

BETHANY. Bambi.

CHANCE. I was gored to death by Bambi. Go figure. Is that what happened? *(She won't answer.)* Annie?

BETHANY. A deer antler ripped you open from stomach to neck. You managed to make it back here, dial nine one one. But you bled to death before the ambulance got here. God I need a cigarette.

CHANCE. Try the desk drawer.

*(She starts to, then catches herself.)*

BETHANY. Damn it. I don't smoke anymore. I quit.

*(She unwraps a stick of gum. Chews hard.)*

CHANCE. Why?

BETHANY. Not part of my life anymore.

CHANCE. A few cigarettes aren't gonna kill you. How many times have I told you?

BETHANY. Well you're not here to make the decisions Chance. I have to do that all by my little self.

CHANCE. That doesn't sound like you. You've changed. You lost a lot of weight. You look great.

BETHANY. Stop and think girl. You're having a conversation with your imagination. Your subconscious must be trying to tell you something. Find out what. What are you doing here?

CHANCE. What are *you* doing here?

BETHANY. It's not supposed to work this way. I ask the questions, you answer.

CHANCE. I'll answer when you answer.

BETHANY. Okay. Floyd and I are only here —

CHANCE. Floyd?

BETHANY. — to put the house in order —

CHANCE. Floyd?

BETHANY. — so we can get on with —

CHANCE. Floyd?

BETHANY. Yes Floyd. His name is Floyd. Floyd, Floyd FLOYD.

FLOYD. Yes Bethany?

*(Gulp! BETHANY winces. Geez, she didn't mean to shout.)*

BETHANY. Nothing honey.

CHANCE. You call him honey? Who is this guy?

BETHANY. Nobody of importance to you.

*(FLOYD comes bounding back in. CHANCE gets suspicious.)*

FLOYD. You okay Bethany?

BETHANY. No. Yes.

FLOYD. Do you want to sit down?

CHANCE. This guy looks familiar. I know him, don't I.

BETHANY. No.

FLOYD. You want to lie down?

CHANCE. Are you sure?

BETHANY. Yes.

FLOYD. Alright. Right over here.

*(He tries to guide her to the couch.)*

BETHANY. What? No. I don't want to lie down.

FLOYD. Okay. Standing is good. Anything I can do?

CHANCE. There's a good question.

BETHANY. No, I'm fine. Really.

FLOYD. You're sure?

BETHANY. Absolutely.

FLOYD. Good. Because I wanted to talk to you.

BETHANY. Now?

FLOYD. "Delays have dangerous ends." Henry the fifth. I think we're going about this moving all wrong. We should start with the basement —

CHANCE. I do know him. Who is he? Who is he —

FLOYD. — and then work our way up, labeling each box —

BETHANY. My dentist.

FLOYD. Why would we do that?

BETHANY. Do what?

FLOYD. Label the boxes "my dentist."

BETHANY. Did I say that? Silly me. What I meant to say was you're so smart for a dentist.

CHANCE. *(Bending low and looking up FLOYD's nose.)* Now I recognize you! Only time I ever see him, I'm looking up his nostrils. Don't you think it should be a rule all dentists should have mustaches. Something to block that view —

BETHANY. Oh shut up.

FLOYD. I didn't say anything.

BETHANY. Of course you didn't. You're the silent type. Not like some ...

CHANCE. Wait a sec. What're you doing here with my dentist?

BETHANY. Well he's my dentist now.

FLOYD. Who is?

BETHANY. Who is what?

FLOYD. What?

BETHANY. What? What?

CHANCE. No what's on second. Who's on first.

FLOYD. Maybe we should deal with this later.

CHANCE. Open your mouth.

BETHANY. No.

FLOYD. Okay, we'll deal with it now.

CHANCE. Then he's not really your dentist.

BETHANY. Yes.

FLOYD. Good idea.

CHANCE. Then open your mouth. *(She does. He starts to check her teeth.)* Geez, look at this. He must really love you.

BETHANY. What am I a horse?

FLOYD. Not to me. Bethany, I'm just trying to help.

BETHANY. You are darling.

CHANCE. Darling? You're his darling now? What is he helping you with?

BETHANY. Organize this house. I'm selling it.

FLOYD. I'm trying. That's what the boxes are for.

CHANCE. To who?

BETHANY. Whom. A man named Adam Lucas —

FLOYD. — will be here Monday morning. I remember.

BETHANY. And then we're getting married.

FLOYD. What?

CHANCE. WHAT!?

BETHANY. We're getting married.

FLOYD. I know, I'm counting the days.

CHANCE. Oh no you're not.

BETHANY. Oh, yes I am. *(She grabs FLOYD's hand and races upstairs, calling back over her shoulder — )* I'm selling this house, getting married, and having a wonderful life!

CHANCE. *(Stewing ...)* Over my dead body.


*BLACKOUT*


## Scene 2

*(The coffee mug has been removed, but other than that, things are pretty much status quo. The front door opens again and BETH-ANY reenters. She looks around, trying to see if CHANCE is*

*floating about. She calls in a hoarse whisper so as not to attract
FLOYD.)*

BETHANY. Chance? Chance?

*(Coast is clear, so she signals for CRYSTAL to enter. CRYSTAL
looks like she could never fully embrace the fact that Woodstock
is over. Tie-dye, crystals, beads in her hair. She takes one step
into the room and can't believe her eyes.)*

CRYSTAL. Oh my god. How ... how incredibly ... tacky! I used
to be an interior designer. I had nightmares like this.
     BETHANY. My husband. *Ex* - husband decorated it.
     CRYSTAL. Uh-huh. What, did he lose a bet?
     BETHANY. No, Chance never lost. He was allergic to losing.
     CRYSTAL. So he did this on purpose? As a child, was he fright-
ened by Abe Lincoln? He ever want to be a rail splitter or anything?
     BETHANY. No. He was just ...  ... just ...  ...
     CRYSTAL. A macho shit-head?
     BETHANY. No.
     CRYSTAL. Insecure about his own masculinity?
     BETHANY. No! He's probably the most secure man I've ever
known. He used to climb mountains. Jump out of airplanes, race cars.
     CRYSTAL. A real Grizzly Adams —
     BETHANY. Chance. His name was Chance —
     CRYSTAL. —Gregory Tobias. Born March eleventh in Duluth.
He used to call you Annie.
     BETHANY. *(Taken aback.)* How did you know that?
     CRYSTAL. I'm very good at what I do. *(Bethany is backtrack-
ing across the floor. Frightened and unsure. Crystal crosses to her.)*
Ms. Walker, don't be afraid. I'm not a witch. This isn't black magic.
Think of me as a ... mediator. You did the right thing by calling me.
Please trust me. I can help. *(Crystal walks across the floor, stepping
on a rug downstage. Energy is suddenly sucked from her legs. She
totters, dangerously close to collapse, then retreats from that spot.)*
Hey-hey. That's it. That's where he died, isn't it?
     BETHANY. No. He died over there.

*(She points to the spot where CHANCE first awoke.)*

CRYSTAL. Strange. I get a strong feeling from this. *(She moves to the spot indicated and swoons even more.)* No you're right. It's here. I can feel him. He's somewhere in this house.

BETHANY. You mean he's real?

CRYSTAL. Absolutely.

BETHANY. I was hoping he was just a figment of my imagination.

CRYSTAL. You'd rather be losing your mind than deal with your husband's ghost?

BETHANY. Well ... I um ... I didn't ... What were my choices again? Do you know why he's here?

CRYSTAL. He's caught between worlds. That happens sometimes. People die suddenly and don't know they're dead.

BETHANY. He knows. I told him.

CRYSTAL. Some people are afraid of death. Afraid of the unknown. Understandable, isn't it? Others never see "the light" of heaven. Or Nirvana. Valhalla. Whatever you want to call it. Some get lost along the way.

BETHANY. Well you know men. They'll never stop and ask directions. Drive around for hours before they'll pull into a gas station.

CRYSTAL. I doubt there's a lot of Texaco's in limbo. Maybe he can't choose between worlds.

BETHANY. No. He was always decisive. Always knew exactly what he wanted and found a way to get it.

CRYSTAL. You said he didn't like to lose.

BETHANY. But why now? Why come back, after all this time?

CRYSTAL. Probably because you came back. Do you still love him?

BETHANY. No. No I do not.

CRYSTAL. Maybe he still loves you.

BETHANY. Can you get rid of him?

CRYSTAL. Are you sure you want me to? Love like that is not to be taken lightly —

BETHANY. Yes. I'm sure.

CRYSTAL. I can't get rid of him unless he wants to go. But I can help him see the way. Open the door. I can lead him to water, but he's gotta want to drink. *(Vanishing into the kitchen.)* OH MY GOD!

BETHANY. What?! What is it?!!

CRYSTAL. This cheese is really old. *(Coming in again, she's helped herself to a banana.)* Do you understand?

BETHANY. Yes.

CRYSTAL. Once he enters ... for lack of a better word .... utopia, I get three thousand dollars.

BETHANY. But I've already paid you a thousand.

CRYSTAL. Yeah, well, that was just to show up. I'm up. That money is non-refundable. I used to be an apartment manager. So just think of it like a security deposit.

BETHANY. Big deposit.

CRYSTAL. Yes it is. But this isn't like calling a mechanic to come fix your spark plugs. I have a talent. A gift that has cost me more than you can possibly imagine. Believe me when I tell you, you're getting a bargain. *(Crystal whips out a big Havana cigar. Chomps off the butt and blazes up.)* Do you mind if I smoke? I used to smoke those little coffin nails. Then I moved up to these big industrial rivets. Worked in a cigar factory for a while, got hooked. Alright, down to business. From now on, you don't talk to him. Anything you have to say to each other, comes through me. I am the mediator. That's very important, do you understand?

BETHANY. Yes.

CRYSTAL. Secondly. I'm going to need to spend some time with him. Alone. In this room.

BETHANY. Why?

CRYSTAL. He died in here. It'll be easier to get him on his way. You don't have to understand. Trust that I'll take care of it. Go on. Let me get my things and go to work.

BETHANY. How long will this take?

CRYSTAL. Not long.

BETHANY. Good. The quicker the better.

*(BETHANY takes off upstairs, and CRYSTAL heads out the front door. A few seconds later VERNA comes out and resumes her*

*search of the place, talking to — )*

VERNA. Harold. Bethany must think we're stupid. Expecting us to believe she can talk to her dead husband. Have you ever heard of anything so ridiculous. She's hiding something. But *your* son won't listen to me. Oh nooooo. She's got him blinded. He needs proof. I'm going to have to find whatever it is ...

*(She keeps looking when Crystal comes back in with a suitcase.)*

CRYSTAL. Hi.
VERNA. Ahhhhhh! Oh.
CRYSTAL. Hello.
VERNA. Who are you?
CRYSTAL. Crystal. Who the hell are you?
VERNA. Verna. What are you doing here?
CRYSTAL. What are *you* doing here?
VERNA. I asked you first.
CRYSTAL. You were doing something.
VERNA. No I was — I mean — Who did you say you were?
BETHANY. Crystal! *(Charging into the room.)* Verna's not up there, she must be —
CRYSTAL. Right here.
BETHANY. *(Gulp.)* Hi Verna.
VERNA. Bethany. Who's the moon child?
BETHANY. Oh, this is Crystal Devereaux. She's ummm ... an-old-friend-who-I-haven't-seen-in-years-and-just-happened-to-run-into-at-the-market-this-morning.
CRYSTAL. Ms. Walker. Either we do this honest —
BETHANY. *(To Verna.)* Excuse me. *(She drags CRYSTAL out of earshot.)* Look, help me out here. I mean if they found out I used the yellow pages to find a voodoo lady to exorcise the spirit of my dead husband —
CRYSTAL. I don't do voodoo.
BETHANY. You know what I mean —
CRYSTAL. It's not voodoo.
BETHANY. No. It's not. I'm sorry, I just —

CRYSTAL. Not voodoo.

BETHANY. Alright. I got it. Okay. NOT VOODOO, geez. I'm just saying that Floyd and Verna can't see Chance. They think this is all in my head. So, just play along. Please.

CRYSTAL. Okay. But keep her out of this room, so I can work.

VERNA. What are you two whispering about?

BETHANY. Nothing. We weren't whispering.

VERNA. I couldn't hear you.

BETHANY. That doesn't mean we were whispering. I — *(Yelling loudly upstairs!)* JUST A MINUTE!

VERNA. What was that?

BETHANY. Floyd was calling us.

VERNA. I didn't hear anything.

CRYSTAL. I did.

BETHANY. See? You might want to get your ears checked.

CRYSTAL. I think Floyd wants you two upstairs. You guys go on. I'll be fine down here. Alone.

VERNA. *(Suddenly very suspicious and not about to leave.)* You go on Bethany. I think I'll stay *right here.* Have a drink, maybe put my feet up.

BETHANY. *(Trying desperately to wrangle VERNA out of the room. Ain't happening.)* You can put your feet up upstairs.

VERNA. Where did you two say you met?

CRYSTAL. Frozen foods.

VERNA. I mean before that.

CRYSTAL. College?

BETHANY. Upstairs is a much better feet upping place.

VERNA. Which college was that?

CRYSTAL. Berkeley.

BETHANY. Stanford.

CRYSTAL. Stanford.

BETHANY. Berkley. *(Uh-oh.)* I'll get you some water from the bathroom.

VERNA. I'd like something cold.

BETHANY. It's cold. We have a refrigerator upstairs.

VERNA. There's no refrigerator up there.

BETHANY. No. Maybe you could help me pick out a place for

one.

VERNA. Why do you want a refrigerator in a house you're selling?

BETHANY. The new owner insists. He ... He has insomnia and likes cold ... cheese in the middle of the night sometimes —

VERNA. What are you babbling about? You're acting very strange. FLOYD!

BETHANY. No, I'm fine. Really —

VERNA. Floyd! There's a stranger down here!

CRYSTAL. I'm not a stranger. In fact Ms. Walk — Bethany's told me so much about you. I feel like I already know you Vera.

VERNA. Verna.

CRYSTAL. Of course. Crystal.

VERNA. Groovy. I'm sorry, I'm having trouble with my ears. Which college did you say?

CRYSTAL. Stanford.

BETHANY. Berkeley.

CRYSTAL. Berkeley. That's right. It was Berkeley. I went to so many it's hard to keep track.

VERNA. You went to more than one college?

CRYSTAL. I went to eleven different colleges.

VERNA. You got kicked out of eleven colleges?

CRYSTAL. No. I left on my own.

VERNA. Couldn't commit?

CRYSTAL. I don't like to be tied down.

VERNA. What do you do for a living?

BETHANY. NOTHING! She doesn't do anything. Do you?

CRYSTAL. I've had lots of jobs. I don't —

VERNA. — like to be tied down. How sad.

*(Instant dislike between these two. Bethany tries to break the mood, crossing to the bar.)*

BETHANY. How 'bout that drink? I'll bring it upstairs to you.

VERNA. So. Do you live around here Crystal?

CRYSTAL. Ahhhhhhh ... *(To Bethany.)* ... do I live around here?

BETHANY. No. Isn't that a coincidence? She was just passing

through on her way to.....

CRYSTAL. Alaska? —

BETHANY. Okay. You know Alaska reminds me of salmon. How about some sandwiches. Can you help me Verna?

FLOYD. Somebody call me?

BETHANY. Floyd, what are you doing here? Let's go upstairs.

FLOYD. Wow, you must be feeling better.

BETHANY. Yes. You were right. A good night's sleep was all I needed.

FLOYD. *(Noticing Crystal.)* Oh, hello.

CRYSTAL. Howdy.

VERNA, *(Grabbing Floyd's arm and dragging him from earshot.)* This is Crystal Devereaux. I don't know what's happening here, but something fishy is going on.

FLOYD. Mother. I think they can hear you. *(To Crystal.)* Hi, I'm Floyd.

VERNA. She's an old friend of Bethany's. From her past.

FLOYD. Really?

BETHANY. Very distant past. An old, uninteresting friend.

VERNA. We were beginning to wonder if she had one.

CRYSTAL. A friend?

VERNA. A past. Tell us more about it. Floyd honey, sit right next to me. I think you'll find this ... enlightening. Now Crystal, tell us everything about our Bethany.

CRYSTAL. Well, there's not much to tell.

VERNA. Oh, come on.

CRYSTAL. No. Really, you probably know more about her than I do.

VERNA. I doubt it.

BETHANY. Anyone up for coffee?

CHANCE. *(As he comes racing down the stairs --)* Annie. Annie! Look at this. I'm up in the attic going through my old trophies and I'm covered in dust. Dust! How does a ghost attract dust?

*(He's right in her face now, pounding his clothes, sending up a tiny puff of attic-powder as evidence. BETHANY instantly tenses at his appearance. FLOYD starts to sneeze from the dust which*

*makes BETHANY whimper as she tries to pretend nothing's wrong.)*

VERNA. Gesundheit. Bless you. *(He keeps sneezing.)* Uh-oh.

*(He digs in his pocket. Resurfaces with an asthma inhaler and takes a hit. It calms him a bit.)*

FLOYD. I'm alright. I'm fine. Like Sophie Tucker said, "keep breathing." *(Noticing BETHANY has gone rigid.)* Are you alright. Bethany?
VERNA. She looks terrible. Look, she's so rigid.
CRYSTAL. She's fine, just a little tight.
VERNA. Tight? She's stiff as a board. I could do my ironing on her.
CRYSTAL. You're fine, right Bethany?
BETHANY. *(Understanding CRYSTAL's firm gestures, she breaks into a parody of a loose puppet.)* Fine. Yes. Loose as a goose. Fine.
VERNA. She's not fine. Maybe she thinks she's being haunted again.

*(BETHANY whimpers again, trying to ignore the ghost.)*

CHANCE. Haunted? Haunt — yeah, that's us. Topper and Mrs. Muir. Ooooooooohhhhhh. That's right Ebenezer, you're being haunted by the ghosts of dead husbands past.... ....and dead husbands yet to come. *(Noticing CRYSTAL, he crosses to her, examining her up and down.)* Who's this?
CRYSTAL. Bethany. Go get us that coffee.
CHANCE. Annie, I asked you a question.
CRYSTAL. Coffee Bethany.
BETHANY. Yes. Right. Good idea. Floyd, would you like coffee?
FLOYD. Um. I don't know. Is anybody else having some?
CHANCE. Bethany?
BETHANY. Oh, you know, I'm not sure I have any.

CHANCE. Damn it Annie. Don't you ignore me. Don't you dare ignore me! *(Just as he takes a threatening step toward BETHANY, CRYSTAL steps into his path. That throws him. He tries to sidestep again, and again she blocks him. He's thrown.)* You can see me?!

*(Again he tries to sidestep. Soon they're both dancing back and forth. VERNA and FLOYD are staring at her like she's nuts.)*

FLOYD. Are you alright?

VERNA. Ms. Devereaux. You seem rather antsy. Do you need to use the bathroom?

CRYSTAL. No. I'm fine. Just a little keyed up —

CHANCE. Bullsh—

CRYSTAL. Maybe I should just — *(To CHANCE.)* SIT DOWN AND SHUT UP — *(He does. She turns innocently back to VERNA.)* — for a moment.

BETHANY. I can't find any coffee.

VERNA. Well. I think we brought some. Must still be with the groceries in the trunk of the car. We'll just see. Come on Floyd.

*(FLOYD obediently moves to help his mother. She stops in the doorway, speaking in a loud whisper, not caring who hears ... )*

VERNA. Something is wrong here. Definitely wrong. The Galaxy Queen didn't just pop up as coincidence. She's after something. I don't know what, but I can smell it. *(Pointing to her nose.)* This doesn't lie.

FLOYD. No. You have a very honest nose. Most of your orifices have admirable qualities. Can we talk outside, please.

*(They vanish. Once CHANCE is sure they're gone he turns to BETHANY and CRYSTAL — )*

CHANCE. Alright, just what the hell is going on here? Who is this and what's she doing here?

CRYSTAL. Crystal Devereaux. I'm here to help you on your way.

CHANCE. You can see me.
CRYSTAL. Yes. Bethany, can you leave us alone.

*(Bethany starts for the door.)*

CHANCE. Annie. Don't go.
CRYSTAL. Yes, go.
CHANCE. No.
CRYSTAL. Please. I need to talk to Chance alone.
CHANCE. Look, lady. I got nothin' to say to you. I want to talk to her.
CRYSTAL. You want to talk to her. You talk to me. Bethany, please leave us.
CHANCE. No Annie! *(BETHANY tries to leave. CHANCE follows her but CRYSTAL stabs out her foot, tripping CHANCE. He falls into the floor, then bounces up hopping mad. Until it dawns on him what just happened.)* What the hell's wrong with you?! Are you crazy — Wait a second. You touched me. You made actual physical contact with me. How'd you do that?
CRYSTAL. I didn't. You did. You're gaining substance.
BETHANY. How is that possible? He's dead.
CHANCE. I've always been a quick healer.
CRYSTAL. You don't belong in this world, alright? The longer you stay here, the more ... "real" you're going to become.
CHANCE. Does that mean Doctor Loser and his mother will be able to see me?
CRYSTAL. Eventually, probably yes.
CHANCE. I'll be able to move objects? Like lift rugs and open doors?
CRYSTAL. Yes. The longer you stay, the easier that will be. And the harder it will be to leave. If you wait, you may never get to heaven.
CHANCE. You mean I could stay here forever?
CRYSTAL. Why would you want to stay? She's getting married. Selling this house. You'd be trapped with a bunch of strangers.

*(Suddenly CHANCE is thinking. Thinking hard. Then he turns to —)*

CHANCE. Bethany. I have something to say to you. *(BETHANY doesn't respond. At all.)* What's the deal, can she hear me or not?

CRYSTAL. Bethany, please leave us. He and I have to talk.

CHANCE. Wait. I have something to say to Annie. Just let me say it, then I'll listen to whatever you have to say.

CRYSTAL. Alright. But you talk through me.

CHANCE. Look Annie. I don't want to be the bad guy here.

CRYSTAL. He says he doesn't want to be a jerk.

CHANCE. I didn't say jerk. I said bad guy.

CRYSTAL. Same thing.

CHANCE. No it's not. What are you a thesaurus?

CRYSTAL. No. But I used to work for one.

CHANCE. Yeah, well Ms. Roget. Just tell her what I'm saying word for word. Exactly verbatim. Okay?

*(BETHANY tries to make a hasty exit when —)*

CRYSTAL. I love you, Annie. *(That freezes BETHANY in her tracks. CHANCE is whispering to CRYSTAL, so we don't hear what he says. Only the words as CRYSTAL relates them verbatim to BETHANY. But all three have their backs to the door, and no one realizes that FLOYD and VERNA have reentered, groceries in tow. They freeze when they hear what appears to be CRYSTAL's heartfelt appeal.)* I love you. I've always loved you. I always will. I've never loved another woman. I'd give you the moon and the stars. I came back for you Annie. We were meant for each other. I don't want to lose you, not to this bozo. Don't marry him. I'm not leaving until you agree to stay with me forever. *(BETHANY breaks into tears and races upstairs. CHANCE runs after her, leaving a befuddled CRYSTAL to yell --)* Hey! Hey, you promised to hear me out.

*(CRYSTAL races after them. Suddenly there's a heavy wheezing sound. FLOYD steps back into view, gripped in a heavy asthma attack. He drops the groceries, fishes out his inhaler and sucks. And sucks. And sucks…. VERNA staggers out assessing this new info. Just the excuse she was looking for … )*

VERNA. Did you hear her? Did you? I knew there was something wrong with that woman. My god, this generation. In our day there was none of this boy-boy, girl-girl thing. This whole world is going straight to hell. It's why Rome fell. Well, that's it. Your fiancé is in love with another woman. This wedding is OFF!


*BLACKOUT*


### Scene 3

*(BETHANY is skittering across the room like a pat of butter on a griddle, trying to avoid the heat. FLOYD is following every move she makes.)*

BETHANY. I don't understand what this is all about.
FLOYD. It's a simple question Bethany.
BETHANY. I know it's a simple question.
FLOYD. And I'd like an answer.
BETHANY. I just don't know why you're asking it.
FLOYD. Yes or no.
BETHANY. Yes or no what?
FLOYD. Can you answer my question with a yes or a no.
BETHANY. Maybe.

*(That's when VERNA comes huffing in, luggage in tow. She's moving them out! She drops the suitcase by the front door with a loud THUNK! Both BETHANY and FLOYD stop everything to stare at her. Once she has their attention, she just harumphs and marches upstairs. FLOYD pulls BETHANY to the couch for a quiet, serious talk.)*

FLOYD. Once and for all Bethany. Do you love me?
BETHANY. What kind of question is that?
FLOYD. An honest one, that deserves an honest answer.

BETHANY. Floyd, I think you're being silly.

FLOYD. That's not a yes or no.

BETHANY. I feel the same way about you I've always felt.

FLOYD. That's not a yes. *(And a several ton wall of sadness slams into him as he realizes what he's up against.)* You really don't. Then why did you agree to marry me?

BETHANY. It's complicated.

FLOYD. How complicated. Two people are in love, they get married.

BETHANY. Love is overrated. Marriage isn't about love. There's respect. Trust. Stability. You're a very sturdy man Floyd.

FLOYD. Sturdy?

BETHANY. Our future will be very secure. We won't have to worry —

FLOYD. That's what you think of me? I'm durable. *Paint* is durable.

BETHANY. So is a rock. But it's strong. You can build on it.

FLOYD. Rocks are boring.

BETHANY. Sometimes ...

FLOYD. You think I'm boring?

BETHANY. No, I didn't say that — *(Just then VERNA reappears and drops another load by the door. THUNK! But nobody looks this time.)* It's just that — *(Verna picks it up and drops it louder. THUNK!! Still nobody looks.)* What am I trying to say? *(THUNK!!!)*

FLOYD. What is it mother? What's wrong?

VERNA. Nothing's wrong. I'm fine. Excuse me.

BETHANY. Verna wait. Please. Verna. *(Verna keeps moving.)* Verna. Can she hear me?

VERNA. No I can't hear you.

BETHANY. You must've or you wouldn't have answered me.

VERNA. Floyd, tell her I have nothing to hear from her.

FLOYD. I think *she* can hear *you* mother.

VERNA. Tell her.

FLOYD. She has nothing to hear from you.

BETHANY. Then at least talk to me. Tell me what's bothering you.

VERNA. I couldn't hear that.

BETHANY. Tell her.

FLOYD. Bethany wants you to tell her what's bothering you.

VERNA. I have nothing to say to that woman. Get your things Floyd, we're leaving. Right now.

BETHANY. Leaving. Floyd no. Please don't go. Verna. *(But VERNA's marching up the stairs, ignoring her.)* Verna please. Talk to me. Tell me what's going on. Verna. Verna.

FLOYD. Mother, talk to her.

VERNA. I've nothing to say to her.

BETHANY. Verna.

VERNA. Floyd.

FLOYD. Bethany. Mother.

*(And all three vanish up the stairs calling each other's names when CHANCE comes in the front door, CRYSTAL on his heels — )*

CRYSTAL. Chance. Chance. Do you believe me now? You just saw for yourself that you can't leave this property. You died here. You'll never be able to go beyond the fences of your land.

CHANCE. That's still seven and a half acres. Plus this cabin. What else do I need?

CRYSTAL. You can't be serious. You actually want to stay?

CHANCE. What am I supposed to do, just quit? Give up my house, my life, Annie. I don't lose that easy.

CRYSTAL. *You're dead,* for God's sake.

CHANCE. I'm not going to let a little thing like that beat me.

CRYSTAL. I think you're missing the basic function of what dead people do. They move into the afterlife. Down that long dark tunnel, toward that warm glowing light into heaven.

CHANCE. What if you didn't see a tunnel or light?

CRYSTAL. You didn't see it?

CHANCE. I'm not saying that. It's just, how are you so sure it leads to heaven? What if you've made mistakes?

CRYSTAL. What mistakes have you made? What happened when you died?

CHANCE. I'm talking hypothetical. Did Hitler see the same

light? Did Stalin? And how do you know that spending eternity with Annie isn't heaven? I know it would be for me.

CRYSTAL. You must love her a lot.

CHANCE. More than you can know. If love were real estate, I'd be Asia.

CRYSTAL. Look bub, you are costing me three thousand dollars by not doing what you should be doing. So why don't you just move your ass along, let me get my cash and blow outta here.

CHANCE. No.

CRYSTAL. Please, just try it once. If you don't like it, you don't have to go. But once you see it, I think you'll want to. Unless you're afraid.

CHANCE. I'm not afraid of anything.

*(He's trying to move a potted plant.)*

CRYSTAL. I think you are.

CHANCE. You're crazy. A nut bar. *(CRYSTAL clucks like a chicken, taunting him.)* Alright Houdini. I'll try it on one condition. If I don't like it, you gotta help me learn to stay. Teach me to move objects. Open doors and stuff.

CRYSTAL. Alright, deal. *(Crossing to him. Getting very close. Nearly hypnotic.)* Open yourself up to it. Close your eyes. Relax. Take a deep breath. *(He takes a sarcastic gulp. She grabs his nose and pinches hard. OW!)* Are you going to breathe? *(He nods, and does.)* And open up your heart. That's all there is to it. Let it into your heart. Can you feel the peace? Tranquility. Tranquility.

CHANCE. I feel like an idiot.

CRYSTAL. *(Pissed, she grabs his lapels and invades his face.)* Look pal, you will feel peace and tranquility or I'm gonna break both your knees. Got it?!

*(So he tries again. After a few seconds to get tranquil, a light begins to glow from high on the stairwell. Gentle at first, then gaining strength. It gets brighter. Stronger. Until it's an impossibly pure white beacon overpowering everything. Calling to him. His throat goes dry. But as the light gains strength, CRYSTAL*

*winces. Then rubs her temples. A nut with a sledge hammer is
loose inside her skull. CHANCE starts to walk toward it in awe.
Then at the last second -- )*

CHANCE. Nope. No way. Huh-uh. I'm not going. Forget it.

*(The light fades. Crystal crumples holding her head.)*

CRYSTAL. What did you see out there?
CHANCE. Nothin'. I didn't see anything.
CRYSTAL. Nothing? Are you telling me there's nothing out
there?
CHANCE. I didn't see anything.
CRYSTAL. You must've.
CHANCE. Nope.
CRYSTAL. Please, it's important to me. I've got to know.
CHANCE. Can't help ya. Sorry. Let's get started.
CRYSTAL. Leave me alone. I have a headache. *(She grabs a
bottle of vodka, yanks the top and gulps straight from the neck.)* You
had no intention of going, did you?
CHANCE. *(Shrugging.)* Deal's a deal and you lost. You gotta
teach me to move stuff. You know how, don't ya. Why do you know?
Come to think of it, why is it you can see me when no one else can?
CRYSTAL. Bug off.
CHANCE. Not until you teach me —
CRYSTAL. Alright come on. *(She marches to the front door and
opens it.)* Come on, let's go.

*(So CHANCE follows her gesture and walks outside. CRYSTAL then
just slams the door, locking him out there, and staggers back
into the room. From outside -- )*

CHANCE. Ha-ha. Very funny. Let me in. Okay, big joke. Crystal! I can't open this door. Let me in. I'm not kidding!

*(But CRYSTAL just takes another long pull on the vodka. Half the
bottle. She sets it on the end table, and collapses into the sofa,*

*rubbing her throbbing head. FLOYD comes in. Angered. He sees her down there, vulnerable and oblivious to him. The woman that's destroying his life. He sneaks up behind her, grabs the vodka bottle and raises it like a club — and freezes. He'd like nothing better than to smash her skull in. But he's a lot more Jeckle than Hyde. The goodness in him prevents him from doing it. So he stands there, going through these contortions as the inner battle rages until -- )*

CRYSTAL. Floyd!

*(He freezes. He tries to act nonchalant, improvising a way out. He stares at the bottle, contorted above his head.)*

FLOYD. Look at that. That's, that's a good year. Huh? What're you doing?
CRYSTAL. Nothing. What are *you* doing?
FLOYD. Nothing too. Probably even more nothing.
CRYSTAL. Oooh, my head. You wanna do me a favor and hit me?
FLOYD. Huh?
CRYSTAL. The bottle. Hit me. Please.
FLOYD. You want me to hit you?
CRYSTAL. You got the bottle, don't ya?
FLOYD. Yes, but —
CRYSTAL. Then do it. *(His pleasure. He raises it like a club again, but again he can't do it. Then CRYSTAL thrusts out a glass. Oh yeah. Fill it.)* Thanks. My head is killing me.
FLOYD. Maybe I can help.
CRYSTAL. I don't think so.
FLOYD. Let me try. Put your head down. *(He forces her head down hard and starts massaging her neck.)* So, Crystal. Tell me about yourself. Married? Have a boyfriend?
CRYSTAL. No.
FLOYD. Big surprise.
CRYSTAL. What?
FLOYD. Keep your head down. I was saying I was surprised. I

would think lots of *men* would like to be with you.

CRYSTAL. I've never really had a boyfriend.

FLOYD. Well maybe you should give them a chance. After all you're smart, independent, strong, witty. Adventurous. Beautiful. I would think lots of *men* would give anything to be with you. Some may even leave their fiancées. Just cast 'em aside like old garbage cause they can't love them ...

*(During the above he's been massaging harder and harder. Now he's practically strangling her.)*

CRYSTAL. Ouch. Floyd. Hey, that hurts.

FLOYD. Oh. Sorry. *(He calms, gently massaging again.)* You have a lot to offer Crystal. Maybe it's time you gave men a chance. How's that?

CRYSTAL. *(Craning her neck around. Surprised.)* Gone. Headache's gone. No one's ever been able to do that before. How'd you do that?

FLOYD. Relaxation technique I use on my patients sometimes. So what do you say? About men. I'm sure there are thousands that would give anything to be with you. Even for a short time.

CRYSTAL. Well, if the right one ever came along ...

FLOYD. Maybe he has already and you just haven't noticed.

*(They smile and there's an actual moment of connection. CRYSTAL is seeing FLOYD for the first time. Really seeing him and liking it. At that second CHANCE jumps in front of the window. He's bouncing around outside like a kid on a pogo stick. Waving his arms, trying desperately to get CRYSTAL's attention. She sees him — )*

CHANCE. OPEN THE DOOR.

*(CRYSTAL just walks over to the window and pulls the drapes, seal-ing CHANCE outside. She turns thoughtfully to FLOYD -- )*

CRYSTAL. Tell me about yourself Floyd.

FLOYD. There's not much to tell.

CRYSTAL. Now *you're* being modest. What do you do for a living?

FLOYD. I'm a dentist.

CRYSTAL. You have your own practice?

FLOYD. No. I work for a conglomerate. Most independent practices fail within the first three years. It's a tremendous risk. Tremendous. Confucius said, "The cautious seldom err."

CRYSTAL. You read a lot, don't you Floyd.

FLOYD. Yes. You can learn a lot from other people's adventures.

CRYSTAL. What about your own adventures?

FLOYD. I can't afford many.

CRYSTAL. You're a dentist, that's good money —

FLOYD. That's not what I mean. I can't afford to take risks, I have too many responsibilities. Since my dad died it's been just me and my mom. Someone had to take care of us.

CRYSTAL. How old were you?

FLOYD. Twelve.

CRYSTAL. You were a breadwinner at twelve? Didn't you miss bein' a kid? Hangin' out with the gang?

FLOYD. It was a trade off. My mom was my best friend. And I always figured there'd be a time when adventure was —

CRYSTAL. Safe?

FLOYD. Yeah. Does that sound boring?

CRYSTAL. The way I see it life is like a candle, lit the moment we're born. You can hide it in the corner, sheltering it from the elements, hoping it will just burn down to a stub. Or you can plant it on a mountain and let it shine like a beacon to the world. Taste the wind and rain. Either way, they're both going to burn out. So I keep burning. If a job gets too dull, I try a new one. I don't like where I live, I stick my finger in an atlas and I'm outta here.

VERNA. *(Coming in with the last of their things, Bethany dogging her heels.)* Floyd, we are out of here.

BETHANY. Verna, please. This is ridiculous. We need to talk.

VERNA. Does anybody hear anything? I don't hear anything.

BETHANY. Talk to me. Sooner or later you've got to talk to me.

FLOYD. I'll talk to you.
BETHANY. Oh Floyd, not now.
FLOYD. You want to talk? How about answering my question.

*(But BETHANY's not ready to face that. So she chases VERNA, who is after her son, who of course is stalking his bride to be. CRYS-TAL just watches as the three of them chase each other around the room like blind mice.)*

BETHANY. I can't talk about that now.
VERNA. Floyd.
FLOYD. You said you wanted to talk.
BETHANY. I do want to talk. I want to talk to her.
FLOYD. But she's not talking.
VERNA. Floyd.
BETHANY. Yes she is.
VERNA. FLOYD.
FLOYD. Just a minute mother, I can't talk now. *(Back to BETH-ANY.)* Yes, she's talking, but she's not talking *to you.*
BETHANY. She doesn't need to talk, she can just listen.
VERNA. *(Clamping hands over her ears and singing as she storms upstairs.)* M - is for the many things I gave you. O - is for the, um, only child of my womb. T - is for the ah, torment I am put through ...
BETHANY. Verna!
FLOYD. Bethany.
BETHANY. *(Help.)* Crystal.
CRYSTAL. Floyd. *(She stops him. Then nods to BETHANY to leave.)* Bethany.
BETHANY. Verna!
FLOYD. *(Let me go.)* Crystal. Bethany!

*(He brushes past and starts to follow BETHANY who has vanished upstairs.)*

CRYSTAL. Floyd. Let her be a while.
FLOYD. She needs help. She needs me —

CRYSTAL. Follow some good advice —

FLOYD. And I have a right to know —

CRYSTAL. "This above all . . ."

FLOYD. *(That stops him in his tracks.)* ". . . to thine own self be true." Shakespeare.

CRYSTAL. Give her time to work it out on her own.

FLOYD. *(He thinks, then slumps onto the sofa. After a beat:)* Shakespeare. Why'd you have to hit me with Shakespeare.

CRYSTAL. He's the man. Ever seen where he lived?

FLOYD. No. I was planning to go sometime. Maybe in four or five years.

CRYSTAL. It's great, I've been there twice. Even worked as a maid there once. Look at this. *(She reaches into her purse and whips out a stack of photos. FLOYD looks them over.)*

CRYSTAL. See how small the cottages are —

FLOYD. Who's this in the picture?

CRYSTAL. I don't know, just some guy that walked past. This village —

FLOYD. Who's this?

CRYSTAL. I don't know. But the houses look like gingerbread, don't they?

FLOYD. You're not in any of these pictures.

CRYSTAL. No. I had to work the camera.

FLOYD. Couldn't you ask someone on the street to take your picture?

CRYSTAL. I don't want to interfere. Look at this one —

FLOYD. Wait a second. You went to all these places alone?

CRYSTAL. Sure.

FLOYD. You didn't have a friend that wanted to go with you?

CRYSTAL. Well, I don't actually have that many friends.

FLOYD. Nobody you met while you were there? A waiter. Fellow tourist. Convict on parole?

CRYSTAL. Hey-hey. I got a busy life, you know. I don't have time to cultivate relationships.

FLOYD. Sounds lonely.

*(They find themselves looking into each other's eyes. The mood gets*

*a little warm ...)*

CRYSTAL. I don't get lonely.

FLOYD. I do. *(Beat.)* I know all about lonely. It's like sitting in a dark empty grave with a hunger inside that you can never fill.

CRYSTAL. Sounds like you've had experience.

FLOYD. Oh yeah. And then I met Bethany. And it was like being born. I saw the world through her eyes and it was wonderful. When I'm with her I feel alive, and when I'm not ... I don't know how to taste wind and rain.

CRYSTAL. What?

FLOYD. Her first husband was a lot like you. Smoked, drank, raced cars. He ran his own business. Do you know the failure potential on a sporting goods store? Never bothered him, he loved living on the edge.

CRYSTAL. Maybe that's what Bethany's attracted to.

FLOYD. Yeah.

CRYSTAL. Not all women are. Do you really think I'm beauti— *(But before she can finish that thought, her wrist alarm blares. BEEP-BEEP.)* Wow, look at the time. Excuse me.

*(She heads upstairs. FLOYD goes around, emptying her ashtray into the fireplace. He grabs the vodka bottle and is about to replace it behind the bar. Then stops. Looks at the bottle. Looks around. Studies the bottle again. Then makes a choice.)*

FLOYD. Wind and rain.

*(He heads upstairs, taking the bottle with him. After a moment we hear a door close, then another one open. A few seconds later, Bethany creeps into the room. Looking around for CHANCE.)*

BETHANY. Chance? Chance? *(No answer.)* Thank god. Maybe it was all a bad dream.

*(She marches confidently into the kitchen — And is suddenly backing*

*in again, CHANCE towering over her. All confidence has drained away.)*

CHANCE. How many times have I told you to lock the basement windows? How many times?

BETHANY. I'm sorry, I didn't —

CHANCE. AH-HA! You can see and hear me. I knew you were just faking it before. *(She turns, trying to just walk away.)* Don't you walk out on me. Stop right there. Damn it Annie, you will do as I say!

BETHANY. *(Stopping.)* No. I won't. I don't have to anymore. Crystal!

*(She tries running upstairs. He blocks her.)*

CHANCE. Where you gonna run. *(He tries to run past her but knocks over the hat rack.)* Hey did you see that?! I moved it. Look, I'm coming back.

BETHANY. I don't want you back.

CHANCE. Sure you do. *(CHANCE jumps down and starts poking the hat rack. Every now and again he can make it move. Hee-hee.)* Believe it or not, I am here to help.

BETHANY. I don't want your help.

*(She tries to leave.. He won't let her. She unwraps a stick of gum and chews like crazy.)*

CHANCE. Of course you do. You've never been good at making decisions, darlin'.

BETHANY. Don't call me that.

CHANCE. Why not?

BETHANY. I'm not your darling.

CHANCE. Are you my sweetheart?

BETHANY. No.

CHANCE. My honeybunch?

BETHANY. No.

CHANCE. Then what the hell are you mine?

BETHANY. Nothing.

*(Another stick of gum.)*

CHANCE. You are my wife.
BETHANY. No I'm not.
CHANCE. We had a ceremony. We're married.
BETHANY. Not anymore.
CHANCE. What, did I forget to check the expiration date? What are we, cheese? We took a vow. For better or worse.
BETHANY. I said till death do us part.
CHANCE. And I said I'd love you forever.
BETHANY. And you did Chance. Right up to the day you died. That's forever.
CHANCE. Well then you're into bonus time baby. This is forever and a day.
BETHANY. I don't want it anymore Chance.

*(Another stick.)*

CHANCE. This is nuts. Most women would die for a man that would love them eternally. Fight for them. *(He's getting to her. She softens.)* Annie Darlin', you don't wanna marry this putz.
BETHANY. He is not a putz. He's just nothing like you.

*(Another stick, her mouth is getting full.)*

CHANCE. What's happened to you?
BETHANY. Life — Death. It changes people.
CHANCE. But to marry a man you don't love —
BETHANY. I will grow to love him. Some day we'll be very happy.
CHANCE. Some day? Annie, you can't live your life only for the future. That's ... that's ... that's layaway.
BETHANY. That's all I have.
CHANCE. What about memories?
BETHANY. No.

CHANCE. We had a life together Annie.

BETHANY. I'm sorry. I never loved you Chance. I never did.

CHANCE. I don't believe that.

BETHANY. Well, it's true. I've never loved anyone. Ever.

CHANCE. That's not what you said. It was our seventh date. I counted 'em. The picnic on the cliff. Remember that Annie?

BETHANY. I am not discussing my past with you.

*(More gum.)*

CHANCE. Afraid you'll find the truth? You were wearing that summer dress with the lace. Where'd you get that dress?

BETHANY. I'm not discussing my past with you. I'm not doing it, so stop trying.

CHANCE. Remember the love song on the radio —

BETHANY. *(Her mouth crammed to the max.)* Mob, yoooo mar mo mobber.

CHANCE. What?

BETHANY. *(Spitting out the gum wad into her hand.)* I said, God, you are so stubborn. It's like being with a two year old.

CHANCE. Is not.

BETHANY. Is too.

CHANCE. Is not.

BETHANY. Is everything a competition with you? Grow up.

*(She crams the wad back in her mouth.)*

CHANCE. You used to love the little boy in me. What happened to the little girl I fell in love with.

BETHANY. She never existed. This is the new improved me.

CHANCE. I liked the old, flawed you better.

BETHANY. I don't remember her.

CHANCE. I do. She was a little plumper. She used to get the hiccups every time we'd get romantic.

BETHANY. I don't get them anymore. I'm in control.

CHANCE. Remember those showers by candlelight.

BETHANY. No. I remember all the nights alone —

CHANCE. The flickering light turned your skin into liquid gold.

BETHANY. — waiting for you to come back from some business trip.

CHANCE. The smell of the soap. The feel of your hair ... *(He closes in on her. Manipulating. Seducing. Pulling out all his old tricks. BETHANY is trying to get away, but her resolve is slipping. He's getting to her and she hates it.)* What about stars Annie. Does he like to look at the stars?

BETHANY. What?

CHANCE. Lie on a hill of wildflowers and stare at the stars. Find constellations and rename them. Do you remember the lovers? Named them after us. I saw them last night Annie in the northern sky and I fell in love with you all over again. How can you look up there and honestly say you don't remember us.

BETHANY. I don't look up.

CHANCE. You can't do that Annie, you're gonna bump into walls.

BETHANY. I see fine.

CHANCE. *(He knows he's getting to her.)* Dance with me.

BETHANY. No, please.

CHANCE. You dance like a goddess.

BETHANY. Not anymore.

CHANCE. Yes. Remember dancing on our honeymoon? You got blisters on your feet —

BETHANY. And you carried me back to the room.

CHANCE. We were back dancing the next night. Dance with me again.

BETHANY. No.

*(She steps right to walk around him. He steps right to block her. She steps left. He steps left. Every move she makes, he counters. It's almost like they're ... dancing.)*

CHANCE. Yes. I always know what you want Annie.

BETHANY. Damn it Chance, - HIC - I don't want to dance - HIC-.

*(Oh no. Not the hiccups.)*

CHANCE. There she is. *(HIC)* I recognize that little girl.

BETHANY. No you don't - HIC -.

CHANCE. Welcome back Annie.

BETHANY. I am not back - HIC -. Damn you.

VERNA. *(From offstage.)* Bethany. *(Startling BETHANY, which cures the hiccups.)* Are you down there?

BETHANY. Oh great. Get out of here.

CHANCE. I can't leave you with that woman.

VERNA. Bethany?

BETHANY. You listen to me. You keep your mouth shut. I don't need you making me look crazy.

VERNA. *(Entering.)* I want to talk to you.

BETHANY. Now!? Now you want to talk to me?

*(Through the following BETHANY is trying to ignore CHANCE's interruptions. But it gets harder and harder and this conversation becomes a runaway train.)*

VERNA. Bethany, I'd like to talk to you? Woman to woman.

CHANCE. I've never understood that. How else would she do it?

VERNA. Are we alone?

BETHANY. In what sense? I mean that's such a big philosophical question. Are any of us *really* alone.

VERNA. I mean are my son and your ... "friend" here?

BETHANY. No.

VERNA. Good. Then may I be frank?

BETHANY. Sure.

VERNA. Bethany. Call off this wedding.

CHANCE. I agree with Mom. Good call Mom.

BETHANY. Why?

VERNA. Because my son is a romantic fool. Like his father. He's going to get hurt. Please, I'm asking you to let him down gently.

BETHANY. Why?

VERNA. Because he still loves you.

CHANCE. Maybe he's not so stupid after all.

VERNA. We're not stupid.

CHANCE. See.

VERNA. We know who Crystal is and why she's here.

BETHANY. You do? Then you understand —

VERNA. No, honestly I don't. But I suppose if you are still in love —

BETHANY. I'm not in love with anybody.

CHANCE. Ah, your lips are saying no, but your heart is saying yes -HIC- yes -HIC- yes.

BETHANY. Stop it.

VERNA. What? In my day things were different.

BETHANY. In your day?

VERNA. It was men and women. Everything else was kept private.

CHANCE. Amen.

BETHANY. I have no idea what you're talking about.

VERNA. My son tells me you're not even in love with him.

CHANCE. Really? You told him that?

BETHANY. No.

VERNA. I see. You're in love with somebody else.

CHANCE. She's wild about me.

BETHANY. No. *I've never loved anyone.*

VERNA. Is that supposed to make me feel better Bethany? You married a man you weren't in love with.

BETHANY. I didn't ... I mean —

VERNA. My son is a good man.

CHANCE. Yes he is.

VERNA. Honest. Faithful.

CHANCE. Hardworking. Snappy dresser —

BETHANY. Stop it!

VERNA. Not until I finish. He deserves somebody who will love him. Totally and completely for all time. If you can't, step aside.

BETHANY. I can. I will —

VERNA. You can't. You didn't. You married Chance and you don't love him.

BETHANY. He ... I ... he died.

VERNA. So did my husband, but I keep his spirit alive in my heart because that's what love is.

CHANCE. She's right.

BETHANY. Shut up.

VERNA. Don't talk to me that way. I have a right to protect my son from some uncaring, cold-hearted —

BETHANY. You don't think I can keep someone's spirit alive?!

VERNA. That's right. You are incapable —

BETHANY. Wrong Verna! Dead wrong. You want spirit, well back off baby cause here it is. Your hubby's cooped up in some flower pot, well take a look at mine!

*(Ta-da! Then the moment falls flat. Long beat.)*

CHANCE. Annie. She can't see me.

BETHANY. Well, then do something. Move a candle or possess her body or something.

VERNA. Oh no. Not this again.

BETHANY. Prove that you're here. *(But CHANCE has other ideas. He just stops dead. Unmoving. He'll not cooperate.)* Damn you Chance.

CHANCE. I'm not gonna lose you to this guy. Call off the wedding.

BETHANY. NO!

VERNA. FLOYD!

BETHANY. Don't do this to me.

CHANCE. You love me, you know you do. Admit it.

VERNA. FLOYD, YOU'D BETTER GET DOWN HERE!

BETHANY. No. No, he's here. I can prove it!

ADAM LUCAS. Knock-knock.

*(Everyone turns to see ADAM LUCAS in the door. Affable smile, easy going manner. For some reason, CHANCE backs away from him.)*

CHANCE. You ...

VERNA. Who the hell are you?

ADAM LUCAS. Adam Lucas. I'm the man buying this house.

BETHANY. I didn't expect you so early.

ADAM LUCAS. You said first thing Monday. I was a little anxious, thought I'd drive by when I heard voices.

CHANCE. Don't sell my house to him Annie. Don't do it

BETHANY. It's not your house anymore. You willed it to me.

ADAM LUCAS. Who's she talking to?

VERNA. Her husband.

ADAM LUCAS. Oh, where is he? I'd love to meet him.

VERNA. He's dead.

ADAM LUCAS. *(Picking up Harold's urn.)* Oh. Is this him?

VERNA. No. That's my husband.

ADAM LUCAS. Oh.

CRYSTAL. *(Coming in.)* Hey-hey. What's all the shouting?

BETHANY. Will you please deal with him while I deal with this.

CHANCE. Do not sell this house to him!

CRYSTAL. You promised you wouldn't talk to her without me.

ADAM LUCAS. Who's this?

VERNA. Girlfriend.

ADAM LUCAS. Oh. Her husband's?

VERNA. No.

ADAM LUCAS. Your husband's?

VERNA. No. Hers.

ADAM LUCAS. Oh. Pretty crowded in here for a three bedroom.

BETHANY. Will everybody just be quiet. I need a moment to think!

CRYSTAL. Just sit there and shut up.

CHANCE. Not until she calls off this wedding.

VERNA. FLOYD!

ADAM LUCAS. Who's Floyd?

VERNA. My son — Just relax, I'll get you a program later. FLOYD GET DOWN HERE!

*(And FLOYD does come racing in, empty vodka bottle in tow. He's completely drunk. He's also obviously raided CHANCE's closet, because right now he's dressed just like him. Boots. Flannel. Hunting knife. He pounds in, staggers around and bellows in a pathetic parody of what he thinks BETHANY wants. An adventurer.)*

FLOYD. Hey everybody!

VERNA. Oh my god. Floyd?

FLOYD. Hey-hey big momma.

VERNA. Big momma?

BETHANY. Floyd?

FLOYD. Hey babe.

CRYSTAL. Babe?

CHANCE. Those are my clothes.

VERNA. You're drunk.

FLOYD. And I feel great. I feel ALIVE!

CHANCE. What the hell is he doing?

CRYSTAL. Feeling alive.

CHANCE. Well he's feeling alive in my clothes.

CRYSTAL. Somebody should.

BETHANY. Floyd, what is this?

FLOYD. Hey Annie —

BETHANY. Don't call me that.

FLOYD. You know what we're going to do Annie? We're gonna rent a boat and go sailing. Sail all the way to Europe, what'dya say.

VERNA. No Floyd, you can't. You don't know anything about sailing. You get sea sick in the rain.

FLOYD. So it'll be dangerous. That's what makes it fun.

BETHANY. No. Why're you behaving like this?

FLOYD. It's adventure. We could be hurt. Killed. I don't care. I'm willing to die for you Babe. If we could die in each other's arms I'd be a happy man.

BETHANY. Stop it!

FLOYD. But I thought you wanted —

BETHANY. Get out of those clothes, you look ridiculous. I spent three years trying to get Chance out of my system. Why would I want you to be like him?

CHANCE. *(Blocking her path.)* Because you still love me. Show me. Keep this house. Call off this wedding.

FLOYD. Bethany?

CHANCE. Prove it to me —

FLOYD. Answer me.

BETHANY. *(Snaps. She rolls up her sleeves and holds up her*

*scarred wrists as evidence.)* Alright YES! You want proof? How's that?! Huh? How's that?
    CHANCE. What?
    BETHANY. Right there.
    CHANCE. Right where? I don't see anything.
    BETHANY. Well, they healed up. But they were there.
    CHANCE. What was there?
    BETHANY. The scars.
    CHANCE. What scars?
    BETHANY. Suicide you idiot! When you died, I tried to kill myself to be with you. *(Beat while that sinks in.)* God, I've spent all this time trying to forget that. To put my past behind me. But we can't, can we. You win. This wedding is off.
    CHANCE. Yes.
    FLOYD. No.
    VERNA. Yes.
    CRYSTAL. No.
    BETHANY. Yes.

*(The room falls silent, only thudding heartbeats now. Beat ...)*

    ADAM LUCAS. Did I come at a bad time?


*BLACKOUT*


**END OF ACT ONE**

## ACT II
## Scene 1

*(It's just a few moments later, tensions are still at the lava point. FLOYD is still loopy drunk, his tongue a useless chunk of meat. BETHANY is different now. Calmer. Like a wall has come down. She stands at the desk, calmly pulling out a cigarette. She lights up, completing her transformation back to her old self. Even CHANCE is thrown by this news.)*

BETHANY. Now you know all about my past.

VERNA. I knew she was hiding something. I knew she was keeping a secret from us.

BETHANY. Not from you. I was trying to keep it a secret from *me*. I hoped maybe if I didn't face it, it would go away.

VERNA. Suicide. Do you see *now* Floyd. You could've married a corpse.

CHANCE. Everyone else here did.

CRYSTAL. It was a mistake. Nobody really wants to die.

BETHANY. I did.

CRYSTAL. No.

BETHANY. Yes. I was sixteen when we met. I went right from being Daddy's little girl to Chance's wife. I never had to have a life without him. The first night I was alone after he died, it was time for dinner so I pulled out the roaster. I couldn't decide what to make, so I went to the other room to ask Chance. But he wasn't there, so I just naturally called him at the office. They didn't know what to say. That's when it hit me. He would never be back. I just collapsed in the hall, hugging the Corell roaster with little blue flowers we got for our wedding. I knew that cold porcelain was as close to him as I would ever get again. I never did decide what to eat. After a while, I lost interest in eating anything.

FLOYD. Oh Bethany.

BETHANY. I didn't know when to go to bed. When to wake up. How to plan my day. God, life was so much simpler when you were there. Not as scary as it is now.

CHANCE. Doesn't have to be. I'm here now.

FLOYD. Bethany, that'th all behind you now.

BETHANY. I don't think so.

FLOYD. Bethany, pleath. It is ethpethially thignifigant that you lithen to what I have to thay. Have to thay? Oh my God, my tongue ith dead.

CRYSTAL. No it's not.

FLOYD. Well then it'th theverely wounded. Lithen to me. I thound like daffy duck. Thee thells thee thells by the thee thore.

CRYSTAL. It's just the vodka. Makes everything lazy.

FLOYD. Thith ithn't lathy. It'th comotothe. My entire mouth thould be on life thupport.

*(FLOYD collapses into a chair upstage. CRYSTAL and VERNA dote over him. CHANCE pulls BETHANY downstage, out of earshot.)*

CHANCE. Look at him, Annie. He's a wimp. This is the guy you were gonna leave me for?

BETHANY. I wasn't leaving you. You died.

CHANCE. But I'm here now. We can be together again. Just like we used to be.

BETHANY. No. You're dead.

CHANCE. Feel my hand darlin'. That's me. I'm gaining more substance everyday. Can you feel this?

*(He kisses her. She pulls back, stunned. Touching her lips that felt a spark from long ago. FLOYD crosses to her, CRYSTAL and VERNA taking opposite sides of this tug-o-war.)*

FLOYD. Bethany, I'm tho thorry. I didn't mean to get drunk.

BETHANY. I know.

FLOYD. And thith whole Chanth thing. The way I'm dretthed. I could never be the man he wath.

CHANCE. Ooooh, and the understatement of the year award goes to —

BETHANY. I know.

FLOYD. But you thtill don't want to marry me, do you.

BETHANY. I'm not —

CHANCE. Of course you don't. Tell him that.

CRYSTAL. Stop pressuring her.

FLOYD. I'm not prethuring. I'm juth athking.

CRYSTAL. I wasn't talking to you.

BETHANY. Crystal, please help me.

VERNA. Do you see Floyd? She cares more about "That Woman" than she does about you.

BETHANY. Crystal?

CHANCE. Leave her out of this Annie.

FLOYD. Bethany. Pleath anther me.

BETHANY. I don't know what to do. What to say? Floyd, tell me what to do?

FLOYD. I think you thould do whatever you want. Only you know what'th in your heart.

BETHANY. But I don't know what I want. I don't know what's in my heart —

CHANCE. I do. You want someone to take care of you. To be loved like the oceans love the shore.

BETHANY. I — I mean —

CHANCE. If love were sand, I'm the Sahara.

FLOYD. Bethany?

CRYSTAL. Don't listen to him.

VERNA. Floyd stop it. You're making a fool of yourself. You deserve better than this.

BETHANY. How do I ... what do I ...

CHANCE. Tell him it's over Annie.

BETHANY. I don't know —

CHANCE. I do. Haven't I always known what's best for you? He deserves a clean break. Be gentle, but let him get on with his life. Do it now.

BETHANY. Maybe your mother is right. You deserve better

than me.

FLOYD. I don't want thombody better than you.

CHANCE. That's romantic.

FLOYD. That'th not what I mean.

VERNA. Floyd.

FLOYD. You're all I ever wanted. Do you feel anything at all for me —

BETHANY. When Chance died, I couldn't stand the pain of life without him. So I stopped feeling the pain. I stopped feeling anything at all. I haven't since.

FLOYD. Then give me a chance. Maybe you will love me.

CHANCE. What if you do Annie? What if you give your heart totally and completely to this man? He could die tomorrow.

CRYSTAL. NO.

BETHANY. What?

CHANCE. Think about it. Everybody dies. Do you really want to go through the pain of losing someone you love again? The pain of being left alone?

CRYSTAL. You wouldn't be alone.

VERNA. I suppose you'll be with her forever?

CHANCE. I will. I'm safe Annie. Nothing can happen to me that hasn't already happened. We can grow old together, right here in this house. Just you and I. And I'll never die. Never leave you alone again.

*(And that did it. BETHANY is now convinced.)*

BETHANY. Floyd ...

CHANCE. Tell him.

BETHANY. I'm sorry. I can't go through the pain of losing someone again.

FLOYD. You won't lothe me.

CHANCE. That's what I thought.

BETHANY. I can't risk loving you, because I can't risk losing you.

FLOYD. You're thaying I'm too much of a rithk? You're calling off our wedding, jutht to be on the thafe thide?

BETHANY. If anybody could understand, I thought it would be you.

*(He does. Trapped by his own philosophy. Backfired. He just stands there a moment. Then his stomach roils, threatening to burst. He covers his mouth on the verge of volcanic vomiting.)*

VERNA. Floyd honey? Are you alright?
CRYSTAL. It's the vodka on the return flight.
VERNA. Are you going to be sick?

*(He nods violently. VERNA drapes his arm over her shoulder, tries to usher him to the kitchen. But his knees give and VERNA can't support his weight in a straight line. Off balance he's cork-screwing around his mother like an ox around a millstone. Until CRYSTAL runs up, grabbing his free arm. Together they hustle him into the kitchen.)*

CHANCE. You made the right choice Annie.

*(That's when ADAM LUCAS comes back in, legal papers in tow. CHANCE stands behind his bride, telling her how to behave.)*

ADAM LUCAS. Well, I got all the legal papers out of my car. I just need your signature on a few pages.
CHANCE. You can't sell this house to him Annie. Don't do it.
BETHANY. What?
ADAM LUCAS. Your signature. I know this is a bad time ...
BETHANY. Why?
ADAM LUCAS. Well, from what I heard earlier ...
CHANCE. This cabin has been in my family for generations. It means the world to me. Just tell him you won't sell it.
BETHANY. I'm sorry Mister Lucas. I can't sell this house.
ADAM LUCAS. Escrow closes tomorrow.
BETHANY. Well I ...
ADAM LUCAS. I have a lot of money invested in this.
BETHANY. I know. *(To Chance:)* Maybe we could —

CHANCE. No Annie.

BETHANY. I am sorry.

ADAM LUCAS. I know this is a traumatic time. It's natural to have second thoughts ...

CHANCE. Just tell him no.

BETHANY. No.

ADAM LUCAS. *(Getting dark.)* Listen to me young lady. I have thousands of dollars tied up in this. I do not intend to lose. If I have to bring legal action —

CHANCE. He won't do it.

ADAM LUCAS. I will.

BETHANY. Maybe we could compromise —

CHANCE. Don't back down Annie.

ADAM LUCAS. I have lawyers at my disposal that don't compromise.

CHANCE. Bull. Threaten to go to the I.R.S.

BETHANY. I couldn't.

ADAM LUCAS. Neither will I.

CHANCE. Just do it Annie.

ADAM LUCAS. I don't want to make this harder than it is --

CHANCE. Do it!

BETHANY. I'll go to the I.R.S.

*(ADAM LUCAS suddenly gets scared. And silent. CHANCE kisses BETHANY's hair.)*

CHANCE. Good girl.

ADAM LUCAS. You wouldn't.

CHANCE. Just nod. *(She does.)* Now maybe you'd better go upstairs, darlin'. *(She does. CHANCE crosses to ADAM LUCAS and stares him down.)* I didn't figure you'd want that. Games over. I win. You lose. Close the door on your way out.

*(Cocky and happy CHANCE vanishes upstairs to be with BETHANY. ADAM LUCAS is left on stage a moment, stewing. Then in frustration he slams down the pages. Wanders a moment, trying to figure what to do. Then starts searching the place. Under pil-*

*lows, the fireplace. Searching when FLOYD, CRYSTAL and VERNA reenter.)*

FLOYD. I feel better. At least I can use my tongue again.

*(They all freeze, staring at ADAM LUCAS who is searching. He freezes, trying to look nonchalant.)*

ADAM LUCAS. Um. Ah ... I was looking for a phone.

*(They all point. He follows their gestures to the wall phone and dials. FLOYD slumps to the sofa.)*

VERNA. Don't worry. I think this is all for the —
FLOYD. Best? How do you figure that?
VERNA. Look what just happened. The woman is clearly unstable. My god Floyd, you'd never know what to expect from her.
FLOYD. That's what I love.
VERNA. How can you say that? She's dangerous. If you insult her pot roast is she going to stab you with a fork.
FLOYD. She wouldn't do that.
VERNA. She tried to kill herself. Next time she could take you with her. She should get a job at the Post Office.
CRYSTAL. Verna.
VERNA. Well who knows what she'll do. We need somebody calm. Stable. You deserve a secure future honey.
ADAM LUCAS. Dennis? It's me. She took the house off the market. The house on Ridgeway drive. Ridgeway. R-I-D-G — G. No, G as in gopher. Gopher. G-O-P-H-E-R.
VERNA. She doesn't love you anyway.
CRYSTAL. Up until an hour ago, she couldn't love anybody. It's like she's just been unlocked. Maybe she does love you and doesn't know it yet.
VERNA. Maybe she's psychotic and doesn't know it yet. I'm glad this happened now. Now we can go back to our old life together.
CRYSTAL. What?
VERNA. Just the two of us. We belong to a different time.

ADAM LUCAS. A gopher! The animals that dig holes in your lawn. They're like muskrats with teeth. Muskrats! M-U-S-K-R. R! R as in river. River!

VERNA. We belong back when people had morals. We don't belong here. Pack your things and let's go home.

CRYSTAL. Floyd, don't do this. Do you really want to go back to your old life?

VERNA. We had a wonderful life. We played canasta and Mah Jhonng. The two of us were very happy —

CRYSTAL. Were you? Floyd, I lied earlier. *I do know* what it's like to be lonely. It's horrible. You have a ghost of a chance here. Fight for it.

VERNA. Why do you want him to fight?

CRYSTAL. Cause you're a decent, lovely man Floyd.

VERNA. What do you know about men?

CRYSTAL. There are women who would love to have you. Trust me.

VERNA. What are you, fickle? You won.

CRYSTAL. Won what?

VERNA. Her.

CRYSTAL. Her who?

VERNA. Bethany.

CRYSTAL. What?

ADAM LUCAS. What?

CRYSTAL. What are you talking about?

VERNA. Don't play coy. We know all about you. You're a lesbian —

CRYSTAL. WHAT?

ADAM LUCAS. WHAT?

CRYSTAL. What?!

ADAM LUCAS. A river! Like the Mississippi. Missis-- M-I-S-S-

CRYSTAL. *(Marching over, snagging the phone away--)* He'll call you back. B-A-C-K! *(She slams down the phone and shoves ADAM LUCAS into the kitchen.)* There's a phone in the kitchen. Knock yourself out. Now what are you talking about?

VERNA. We know all about you. We heard you say it. You'd die for her. Give her the stars.

CRYSTAL. Alright, I think I know where we're getting off track here. You misunderstood. This is one big giant misunderstanding. We are not lovers.

FLOYD. It's alright. I understand. There's a lot there to love about Bethany. I know how you feel.

CRYSTAL. Trust me on this big guy, you don't know how I feel. Bethany and I are not lovers. Nada. Nyet. Nowayski. Never were, never will be. *I am not her lover.*

VERNA. Well, thank heavens.

CRYSTAL. I am a psychic to the dead.

VERNA. Oh my God!

CRYSTAL. I just met Bethany yesterday. She hired me to get rid of Chance's ghost.

FLOYD. What?

CRYSTAL. It's true.

VERNA. This is insane!

CRYSTAL. It's not. It's strange, I'll grant you. But Chance's ghost is here.

FLOYD. It's a figment of her imagination.

CRYSTAL. No. He's not in her mind. He's real.

VERNA. He can't be real. Not really real. Men don't come back from the dead to be with their wives.

CRYSTAL. Floyd, listen to me. I have some experience with this. He is here. And getting stronger. His desire to stay in this world is overpowering. I can't get rid of him.

FLOYD. Is this possible?

CRYSTAL. Look deep in your heart. Forget your head. You know he's here. You've felt him, haven't you.

VERNA. No. No, I refuse to accept — Floyd, don't listen to her.

FLOYD. Mother please!

CRYSTAL. You've been in love with Bethany for years. You used to keep her wisdom teeth in your office drawer.

FLOYD. *(Going white.)* How did you know that? I never told anybody that.

CRYSTAL. Except Chance. And he told me.

FLOYD. Yes. But ... Ah ... he could've told Bethany, and then she told you.

CRYSTAL. Would he have done that?

FLOYD. No. He went nuts when he found them. Didn't want Bethany to know how I felt about her. He would've died before he told her. He's real? *(She nods. Beat. FLOYD is now convinced.)* Then I have lost. I can't compete with him. He's twice the man I am.

CRYSTAL. Damn it Floyd, wake up! She's about to commit her life to living with a ghost. My god if you love her at all, you've gotta help her. If you don't have enough self-esteem to fight, try looking at yourself through my eyes. Because I believe in you.

*(That makes up his mind. In an unexpected move he grabs CRYSTAL's face in his hands and plants a wet kiss on her lips. CRYSTAL is left reeling by the display of affection. She's flustered a moment, then sees VERNA staring at her. FLOYD runs upstairs, a nervous VERNA on his heels. CRYSTAL is thrown, not knowing what the hell to do. She grabs her coat and starts for the door when ADAM LUCAS steps out.)*

ADAM LUCAS. Excuse me.

CRYSTAL. Oh, what now?

ADAM LUCAS. I couldn't help but overhear.

CRYSTAL. You were eavesdropping? I thought you were doing a phone-in spelling bee.

ADAM LUCAS. I have one question for you. Is it true? You can talk to the dead?

CRYSTAL. Yes.

ADAM LUCAS. Then I would like to hire you.

CRYSTAL. Sorry. After what's happened today, I don't do this anymore.

ADAM LUCAS. I'll pay you five thousand dollars for ten minutes of your time.

CRYSTAL. *(Stopping.)* Five thousand. That's five hundred dollars a minute.

ADAM LUCAS. Yes. Eight dollars a second.

CRYSTAL. That was fast.

ADAM LUCAS. I'm an accountant.

CRYSTAL. What do I have to do?

ADAM LUCAS. I want to have a conversation with Chance. His ghost is here. I want to talk with him at eight dollars a second.

CRYSTAL. *(After a moment's consideration, she moves to the stairs and sotto yells --)* Chance. CHANCE. Get down here. *(Then to Adam.)* My money —

ADAM LUCAS. When I'm finished. And I have what I want.

CHANCE. *(Coming down. Stopping at the bottom of the stairs.)* What? I'm a little busy — what the hell is he still doing here?

CRYSTAL. He wants to talk to you.

ADAM LUCAS. Is he here?

CRYSTAL. Yes.

CHANCE. I got nothing more to say to him —

ADAM LUCAS. I know about the money. *(Chance goes white. Trying to look casual. Doing a lousy job.)* Ask him where it is?

CHANCE. I have no idea what he's talking about.

*(CHANCE crosses down R.)*

CRYSTAL. He says he has no idea what you're talking about.

*(ADAM LUCAS moves to where he was just a moment before and talks to dead air.)*

ADAM LUCAS. Don't jerk me around boy. I want the money. Right now.

CRYSTAL. Mister Lucas, that's the closet.

ADAM LUCAS. Well, where the hell is he? *(CRYSTAL points. ADAM LUCAS crosses to talk to CHANCE, but again CHANCE moves away. ADAM LUCAS doesn't know this and again talks to no one.)* I know you've got that money hidden somewhere in this house. Just give it to me, and you can keep the damn house. All I want is my money.

CRYSTAL. Wait a minute, what money?

ADAM LUCAS. He knows what money.

CRYSTAL. I don't. What is going on?

CHANCE. That man was my accountant. He's trying to steal

money from me.

CRYSTAL. You're a criminal?

ADAM LUCAS. No, I'm a CPA.

CHANCE. Oh, big difference.

ADAM LUCAS. Ten years I worked for him, he treated me like dirt.

CHANCE. Hey, I gave you a job after retirement age —

ADAM LUCAS. Paid me half salary. *(To the air.)* Did you think I wouldn't find out? You made no provisions for it in your will. So I am entitled to that money.

CRYSTAL. What money? What is going on?

CHANCE. Forget it. That money represents my entire life's work. I'm not just gonna give it away.

CRYSTAL. What money?

CHANCE. It was my future. I'm not going to let a little thing like being dead keep me from having one.

ADAM LUCAS. I am not a fool. I'm nobody's fool!

CRYSTAL. I am asking a question here. What am I, invisible?

CHANCE. No, I am. What're you tryin' to weasel in on my territory now too?

CRYSTAL. No. I just want to know what's going on.

ADAM LUCAS. What's going on? I'll tell you what's going on. This man has been squirreling away money up here. Cold hard cash.

CHANCE. Cash that *I* earned. It was my retirement fund.

ADAM LUCAS. Now it's going to be my retirement fund.

CRYSTAL. How much?

ADAM LUCAS. Seven hundred and fifty thousand dollars.

CRYSTAL. Seven hundred and fifty grand?

CHANCE. Took me my whole life to earn it —

CRYSTAL. You didn't invest it? Get an IRA, or stocks and bonds.

ADAM LUCAS. That's what I said.

CHANCE. Are you kidding? You lose half of it to Uncle Sam.

CRYSTAL. Not if you get a good shelter.

CHANCE. I can never find the right APR.

CRYSTAL. Treasury bonds are nice.

CHANCE. Yeah, but you can't trust stock brokers. Or accountants. They cheat.

CRYSTAL. So this is some macho code, right? Some image thing for you? Take care of yourself like a real mountain man.

CHANCE. This place is as safe as any bank.

CRYSTAL. Not really. You were killed.

CHANCE. By Thumper, can you believe it.

CRYSTAL. He was a bunny.

CHANCE. Whatever.

CRYSTAL. That's why you want to buy this house. Cause you think the money's here?

ADAM LUCAS. Just tell him to give me the money and I'll go away. Nobody gets hurt.

CRYSTAL. Hurt? What are you talking about, hurt?

ADAM LUCAS. I don't want violence.

CRYSTAL. That's it. Excuse me gentlemen, this is a little too intense for me. I'm outta here.

CHANCE. I'm not giving up my life.

CRYSTAL. He says no. Goodbye.

ADAM LUCAS. Don't go.

CRYSTAL. Look, I don't want any part of this. I don't want to be involved. Just give me my five grand and let me go.

ADAM LUCAS. I don't have the money until he gives it to me.

CRYSTAL. Oh for — Forget it. I'm gone.

*(And she's out the door. Leaving Adam to try and fend for himself.)*

ADAM LUCAS. Why do you want the money anyway? Haven't you ever heard "You can't take it with you."

CHANCE. That's why I'm not going. You know I was never sick a day in my life. I ate right, took care of my health. And then — It's not fair. The game's not supposed to work like this. Well Annie and I can live here forever on that cash. This house will be my heaven.

ADAM LUCAS. What did you say? Forget it. I'm going to find that money ...

*(ADAM LUCAS starts scouring the room. Looking here, looking*

*there. He nearly trips over the rug where CRYSTAL swooned
earlier. That's when CHANCE starts to panic.)*

CHANCE. Stop it.
ADAM LUCAS. What the devil ...
    CHANCE. Stop it! *(But ADAM LUCAS won't. He begins to pull
up the rug, tacked into the floor. CHANCE trying to find a way to
stop him. He's running out of time. ADAM LUCAS just about has the
rug untacked —)* Get out of here! *(CHANCE knocks over the hat
rack, right in front of ADAM's nose. Scared, ADAM LUCAS starts to
back away. He crosses stage and WHAM! CHANCE knocks over the
fireplace pokers, which really freaks ADAM LUCAS out. He starts
backing to the door.)* GET OUT!
    ADAM LUCAS. Okay, okay. This isn't over. It's not over.

*(But ADAM LUCAS leaves. CHANCE stands a moment, walks to the
    rug. He stares at it a long time, then squats in front of it. Think-
    ing. Then he reaches out and throws back the now loose rug.
    Good, he smiles. Then tries to lift the trapdoor underneath.)*

CHANCE. Come on. Come on. *(But it won't budge.)* Too heavy.
BETHANY. CHANCE?!
CHANCE. Just a minute.
BETHANY. What are you doing?
CHANCE. Nothing. I'll be right there.

*(He keeps trying to lift.)*

BETHANY. Is anything wrong? I'm coming down —
    CHANCE. NO! Everything's fine. I'm coming. *(Out of time, he
puts the rug back, promising ... )* Soon. I can do it soon.

*(He returns to BETHANY. We're left with a blank stage for a mo-
    ment. Then CRYSTAL comes back in, hands covering her
    eyes — )*

CRYSTAL. Excuse me. Don't mind me. Don't want to hear anything. I just forgot my coat and suitcase. Then I'm gone. Bye. *(But the stage is empty. So she snags her coat and steps on that rug. She swoons again. Energy sucked out of her. She steps off the spot, control coming back. She stares at the rug. Then stoops and lifts it up. Underneath is a trapdoor. She opens it. And comes out a moment later with a small duffel bag. She looks inside and her eyes bug.)* Oh boy.

### *BLACK OUT*

### Scene 2

*(CRYSTAL is kneeling before that open trap door. Her open suitcase next to her. She is wadding the last pages of newspaper and cramming them into the duffel bag. It's full. She tests the weight to see if it feels like the money ...)*

CRYSTAL. That feels about right ... *(So she drops the duffel back into the hole and reorganizes the rug. It looks untouched. Then she reaches into her suitcase and pulls out a wad of bills. Fans them. Likes the sound of ...)* Seven hundred and fifty thousand dollars.

*(Drops it back in her case. Shuts it. And heads for the door. Is just seconds away from a clean getaway when FLOYD creeps painfully down the steps. He's got on dark sunglasses and winces at even the slightest sound. Suffice to say he's in the deepest pit of hangover hell. He notices CRYSTAL leaving and —)*

FLOYD. Where you going?
CRYSTAL. AHHHH!
FLOYD. AHHHHH! Shhhhhhhhh.
CRYSTAL. *(Barely a whisper.)* Sorry. You scared me.
FLOYD. Oh, please. Please don't shout.

*(She shrugs an apology, then slings her purse over her arm, knock-*

*ing a vase off the table. CLATTER!!)*

FLOYD. Arrrrggggghhhh.
CRYSTAL. Sorry. Hangover, huh?
FLOYD. Is that what this is? I thought a porcupine climbed up my nose. Are they fatal?
CRYSTAL. No.
FLOYD. Oh god. You mean I have to live with this?
CRYSTAL. They go away.
FLOYD. I'll give you a thousand dollars to beat me unconscious until it does.
CRYSTAL. You'll be fine. You just need a little peace and quiet.

*(Just then a CAR HORN BLARES outside. FLOYD comes unglued.)*

FLOYD. What is that?
CRYSTAL. Must be my taxi.
FLOYD. I thought there was a barge coming through. *(Seeing her things. Getting worried.)* You're leaving?
CRYSTAL. Yes.
FLOYD. Why?
CRYSTAL. Just 'cause.

*(She turns to go. FLOYD grabs the case. NO! Not the case!)*

FLOYD. Please don't go.
CRYSTAL. *(Grabbing the case back.)* I have to.
FLOYD. *(Grabbing it again. Now we have a tug of war —)* You don't have to. Please, you really don't.
CRYSTAL, Yes, I really do.
FLOYD. Don't.
CRYSTAL. Do.
FLOYD. Don't.
CRYSTAL. Do!

*(She rips the case free.)*

FLOYD. Give me one good reason.

CRYSTAL. I could give you almost a million. But I can't. Sorry.

*(The HORN BLARES again. CRYSTAL turns to the door and shouts — )*

CRYSTAL. SHUT UP! I'M COMING. Sorry.

FLOYD. Were you planning to shoot that driver?

CRYSTAL. No.

FLOYD. Will you shoot one of us at least? Please stay.

CRYSTAL. There's nothing I can do here. If Chance doesn't want to leave, I can't help him.

FLOYD. Then help me.

CRYSTAL. Help you what?

FLOYD. Fight for Bethany.

CRYSTAL. What is it about this woman?! What has she got that makes men come back from the grave. Makes men want to fight.

FLOYD. *You.* You told me to fight.

CRYSTAL. I did? Well stupid me.

FLOYD. I've never stuck my neck out for anything in my life. I don't know how, or even if I can. When I was a kid, there was this big tree at the end of the block. Huge. All the other kids could climb it. I was scared. I always thought one day I'd be man enough to try. They cut that tree down last year.... I look in the mirror and I'm disappointed in what I see. You said I should try looking through your eyes. I could use them now. I can't risk doing this alone ...

*(During this CRYSTAL has softened. She leaves the case and eases in close to FLOYD. They find themselves very close. Very intimate. Lips just inches apart. The moment holds too long ...)*

CRYSTAL. Are you going to kiss me again?

FLOYD. That was ah ... an impulsive reflex.

CRYSTAL. You mean a mercy kiss.

FLOYD. What? No —

CRYSTAL. I've been mercy kissed before. I know a mercy kiss when I get one —

FLOYD. It wasn't mercy. Believe me.

CRYSTAL. So what kind of kiss was it?

FLOYD. What do you mean?

CRYSTAL. I mean the kind of kiss? Was it a flirt? Cuddle? Smack, nuzzle, fondle, snuggle? Kiss goodbye, kiss off. Sunkist?

FLOYD. Friendship kiss.

CRYSTAL. Friendship. That's what I am to you? A friend?

FLOYD. Yes. A very good, good friend.

CRYSTAL. *(Turning to the door, grabbing the case again.)* Yeah, well I got news for you pal. I'm not your friend.

FLOYD. I think you are.

CRYSTAL. I have never been anybody's friend.

FLOYD. Until now.

CRYSTAL. Wrong. *(Stopping again.)* Let's put this friendship thing on a scale. Like a calendar, okay? January first, New Year's Day, is people that have just met. Total strangers. Christmas is like best friends. That puts me somewhere in mid January. Cold early winter. Understand now?

FLOYD. No. Because to me you're more like November. Thanksgiving.

CRYSTAL. Thanksgiving? No way. That's eleven months away.

FLOYD. Not to me.

CRYSTAL. Alright, I'll give you early February. Valentine's Day, how's that?

FLOYD. You're selling yourself short. You're at least Halloween.

CRYSTAL. That's crazy. I'm maybe President's Day. Maybe. At the latest.

FLOYD. Nope. What's between Halloween and Thanksgiving. When's Arbor Day? I think that's what you are, Arbor Day.

CRYSTAL. I don't want to be Arbor Day. I'm nobody's Arbor Day.

FLOYD. Well you're definitely somewhere in the harvest season.

CRYSTAL. Forget that! Look, I've never been past summer solstice to anybody in my life. I am strictly an early spring gal. Preferably before Easter.

FLOYD. Well, Easter is way late this year.

CRYSTAL. Look, I don't want to be your friend, alright?! I don't need the hassle. I don't need anything, or anybody.

FLOYD. Everybody needs somebody.

CRYSTAL. I don't. I've gotten along just fine. I'm a loner —

FLOYD. Who's going to spend the rest of her life alone.

CRYSTAL. Well thank god for small favors, it won't be that long.

FLOYD. What?

CRYSTAL. Nothing.

FLOYD. What did you say?

CRYSTAL. I didn't say anything, I gotta go.

FLOYD. You said the rest of your life won't be that long ... Oooooooohhhhh ... *(Dawning on him.)* Why didn't you say anything?

CRYSTAL. What's to say? Hi, nice to meet you. I'm dying.

FLOYD. But you're so young.

CRYSTAL. Death is the great equalizer. Who said that? Doesn't matter. Shouldn't surprise you. Everybody else around here is dying. This house has got more death around it than Angela Landsbury's house.

FLOYD. How long?

CRYSTAL. Who knows. Tumors are like that. They remain a mystery.

FLOYD. A tumor? That's why you get headaches.

CRYSTAL. Oh yeah. It's done lots of wonderful things to my brain.

FLOYD. Like what?

CRYSTAL. Forget it.

FLOYD. Like what, I'm ... *(It hits him.)* Like allowing you to see the dead. That's why you've been able to see Chance all this time. That tumor has altered your brain somehow. Given you this gift.

CRYSTAL. Gift? I have to set my watch every half hour to remind myself to go to the bathroom. Even if I don't have to go, I go anyway. Because if I don't ... I can't sleep lying down anymore. I have headaches it takes a fifth of vodka to quell. I have to take jobs like this for cash because Visa and Mastercard revoked my credit. You have any idea how hard it is for me to earn any kind of money?

Still sound like a gift to you?

FLOYD. I'm very sorry. My sympathies are with you.

CRYSTAL. What are you, Hallmark? You gonna start doing dorky greeting cards for the terminally ill? "Sorry to hear you're going to die, that really is a bummer. But hurry on to heaven now and have a bitchin' summer."

FLOYD. I didn't know what else to say.

CRYSTAL. What, no little quotes? No brilliant statements by Shakespeare or Churchill?

FLOYD. This is not my fault.

CRYSTAL. You're right, no one's to blame. "Life's unfair." Write that down, you can quote me on it.

FLOYD. Why're you mad at me?

CRYSTAL. Because you've all got endless time and you waste it. Just piss it away like it's never going to happen to you. Well it is. I would give anything, kill anybody for a few more days. Even hours. And there's a woman up there who was willing to throw away her precious, precious life. All for the man she loved. You've got love and you screwed that up too. You guys are surrounded by love.

FLOYD. And you're not.

CRYSTAL. *(Hiding behind a cellophane curtain of bravado.)* No.

FLOYD. Maybe if you stuck around, people could learn to.

CRYSTAL. Could you? *(He says nothing ...)* Well then I guess this is for the best. Who needs love. I've seen what it does. I mean look how broke up she was because Chance died. I don't want to do that to somebody.

FLOYD. So what now?

CRYSTAL. When the going gets tough ...

FLOYD. Don't go.

CRYSTAL. I have a lot of places to go. Things to do. I want to see the world. I gotta keep moving to find the cure for cancer or paint the next Mona Lisa.

FLOYD. You are so full of shit. You're not running *to* anyplace. You're running *from*.

CRYSTAL. You don't know anything about me.

FLOYD. I know you've had a bazillion jobs and a closet full of empty photographs. 'Cause you're terrified.

CRYSTAL. What do you know —

FLOYD. I know you're afraid of dying alone. We all are.

CRYSTAL. I don't want to cause anyone pain.

FLOYD. You're afraid they won't feel pain. You're afraid no one is going to miss you when you leave this planet. So you just run away so you'll never have to find out.

CRYSTAL. Well at least in my running, I'm tasting life. You hide from it. *(Clutching the suitcase.)* I've got a chance now, and I'm taking it. What risks have you ever taken? *(The CAR HORN again.)* I really have to go.

FLOYD. I'll miss you. *(That freezes her in the doorway. But she won't turn. Half a second later, she's gone. FLOYD's left alone on stage a moment, as we hear the car pull away. Then FLOYD bolts, charging out the door after her —)* CRYSTAL!

*(After a beat, CHANCE comes tip toeing down the stairs. He looks around to check his alone-ness. Then crosses to the rug. Takes a moment to summon all his strength and tries to move the rug. IT FLIPS BACK! Elated he tries the trap door. IT OPENS! YES, Yes, yes. This is what he's been waiting for.)*

CHANCE. Come to Poppa. *(He reaches into the hole and comes out with sack, which he thinks is the real money. He cradles it, holding it. Knowing it's —)* Seven hundred and fifty thousand big ones. If I had a dollar for every dollar I have now. I'd have a lot of dollars. *(He laughs gleefully. Then sets the duffel on the sofa and trots back to the stairs. Pulls out yet another fake duffel bag and brings it over. He reaches inside and fans a bunch of different colored money —)* Alright. With seven hundred and fifty thousand of these you can buy a railroad. Or electric company. Or Marvin Gardens with a hotel.

*(Hee-hee. He sticks this new-fake sack back into the hole and covers it up. Then takes CRYSTAL's fake sack and looks madly for a place to hide it. The closet! That's it. He opens the door and enters. A few seconds later he comes back out. Happy with himself. He moves to the window and looks out. Uh-oh, some-*

*one's coming. He scuttles into the kitchen just as FLOYD comes
running back. We see him outside the window in the midst of an
asthma attack. He digs out his inhaler and sucks. Then stares at
it. The talisman of his weakness. In a frustrated howl he chucks
the damn thing into the woods. Gone forever. Then marches out
of sight. That's when Verna comes down, talking to Harold's
urn.)*

VERNA. I am getting us out of here Harold. Once and for all,
we're leaving this nut house. Suicide and witch doctors. People talking to their dead husbands. It absolutely insane. Don't you think? Me
too. *(FLOYD reenters, crossing to the stairs. There's something different in him now. A tired, but calm acceptance.)* Floyd. I've packed
your things. We're leaving.
    FLOYD. Nope.
    VERNA. *(Looped.)* What? What do you mean, nope.
    FLOYD. I mean no.
    VERNA. No? Just no?
    FLOYD. No as in "not so." Adverb used to express refusal, de-
nial, or disagreement. As in "no we are not leaving."
    VERNA. I want to get out of here Floyd. I want us to get back to
our old life —
    FLOYD. What life is that Mother? We don't have a life. We're
the walking dead. Both of us. I'm afraid to live. And you're waiting
around to die.
    VERNA. You're still drunk.
    FLOYD. I hope not. Cause for once things actually seem clear to
me. You know what I learned today? That just being alive is a risk. I
could get hit by a bus tomorrow. Or get a brain tumor —
    VERNA. Don't talk like that.
    FLOYD. Why not, it's true. I've spent my life afraid of making a
mistake. And that's the worst mistake of all. Crystal's right —
    VERNA. Oh Crystal. You can't drink and smoke yourself into
an early grave. You have to plan for tomorrow.

*(The bottom drops out of this conversation for a moment. Then it
races out of control down an unexplored track —)*

FLOYD. And what about today? We hide from it behind dad's memory. You know what else I learned today? You don't like Bethany because she's too much like you.

VERNA. We're nothing alike.

FLOYD. You're identical twins. You're both clutching a ghost, looking at life in a rose colored rear-view mirror and calling it great.

VERNA. In my day —

FLOYD. This is your day, mother. You are alive and taking up space on the planet. You either make an active contribution to change it or keep quiet. You don't get to hide behind that "in my day" crap.

VERNA. IN MY DAY a woman stood beside her husband. For all time. Bethany's right, she's doing the right thing. Keeping her husband's spirit alive —

FLOYD. *(Grabbing the urn, then touching his head and heart.)* Dad doesn't belong here, on display like some creepy shrine. You know where he belongs? Here. And here. But not here.

*(He dumps the ashes all over the floor.)*

VERNA. Floyd!

FLOYD. Let him go mom. If you really love him. Let him go.

*(He drops the urn and races upstairs. VERNA stands a moment, shattered. Then gently stoops and picks up the urn and tries scooping the ashes back inside. Nothing has changed ... Nothing has changed ...)*

## BLACKOUT


### Scene 3

*(It's just a little while later. In the BLACKNESS we hear the sound of a VACUUM CLEANER. As the lights come up we see VERNA vacuuming up all of Harold. After a few moments she shuts the*

*thing off. Then unzips the catcher and removes the bag. It's
plump with Harold's ashes. VERNA clutches it like a baby, trying to gain comfort from its nearness. She wanders the room a
moment, cradling Harold against her bosom. She gently places
the vacuum bag on the sofa, not knowing what to think or do
anymore. After a tense beat, she takes the vacuum into the
closet. And comes out. But something in the back catches her
eye ...)*

VERNA. Wait a minute. What is this?

*(She ducks back inside. Just then there are FOOTSTEPS on the
stairs, and a few moments later, BETHANY and CHANCE come
down. She's smoking again.)*

CHANCE. Nobody here. Maybe they left.
BETHANY. Floyd wouldn't leave without saying goodbye.
CHANCE. I dunno. You don't know his type like I do —
BETHANY. He wouldn't do that. He wouldn't.
CHANCE. Alright. Hey. We're gonna be so happy again.
Thrilled. Raptured. If joy was potatoes, we'd be Idaho.

*(He pulls her close. She hugs him.)*

BETHANY. Well I guess I should start packing.
CHANCE. What?
BETHANY. We may as well start heading back to the city.
CHANCE. The city. No, we can't leave here.
BETHANY. I won't sell this house Chance. We can come back
whenever you want. But my whole life is in the city.
CHANCE. We can't leave here. Ever.
BETHANY. What are you talking about? Why not?
CHANCE. I died here Annie. I can't leave this house. At least
not the property.
BETHANY. Why not?
CHANCE. I don't know. Being dead didn't come with an in-
struction book. I just know we can't leave. You'll have to stay. *(She's*

*not thrilled.)* Come on, it'll be great. Just you and me. Alone. In private.

BETHANY. But there's no schools around here for two hundred miles.

CHANCE. So?

BETHANY. I was going back to school Chance. Getting my degree.

CHANCE. What do you need a degree for? You're perfect the way you are. Perfect. You can get rid of that apartment in the city now —

BETHANY. I just got it all fixed up the way I wanted it.

CHANCE. Okay. You can fix up this place. Anyway you want. Women are good at that kind of stuff.

BETHANY. I suppose it wouldn't be so bad.

CHANCE. No, it'll be great.

BETHANY. We could carpet the floor. Get some lace curtains. Take down the deer heads.

CHANCE. Annie, that was my first kill — Alright, whatever you want.

BETHANY. We can convert the second bedroom into a studio for my paints.

CHANCE. What?

BETHANY. I paint now Chance. Landscapes mostly. Floyd loves them. Even Verna thinks they're pretty good.

CHANCE. Really? Have you sold anything?

BETHANY. Well, no.

CHANCE. Oh. Well, doesn't matter I guess. Important thing is you're having a good time. But this is a small cabin Annie. I don't really think we can afford to lose a whole bedroom for your little hobby. Do you?

BETHANY. Well ... Maybe I could set up in a little corner down here. By the fire —

CHANCE. Annie, paints get into everything. *(Off her expression.)* Alright, how's this. We'll build you a shed out back —

BETHANY. A shed?

CHANCE. Think of it like a studio. You can fool around in there.

*(She smiles, but there's no radiance in it. Just then VERNA comes
blustering back in — )*

VERNA. Bethany. You won't believe what I found in here. I —

*(At the sight of CHANCE, VERNA's eyes go wide in terror. She
stands there pointing. That's all she can do. And for a moment,
she's just a statue of fear. BETHANY is the first to notice.)*

BETHANY. Verna. Are you alright?

CHANCE. She doesn't look so good.

BETHANY. Verna. Verna. Are you okay? Can I get you something?

VERNA. I ... I ... I ...

CHANCE. I. I. I ... Iced tea? Would you like some iced tea? Do
we have any iced tea?

BETHANY. I don't think she wants tea. I think she's trying to
tell us something.

CHANCE. Not doing a very good job. Do you know sign language? Ask her if she knows sign language.

BETHANY. Verna. Come on now. You're scaring me here.
What's going on? How can I help?

CHANCE. How 'bout charades? That's always good, you know,
sounds like ...

VERNA. Ahhhhhhhhhhhhh ...

CHANCE. Ahhhhh? Sounds like Ah? Ba? Ca? Da? Pahk the cah
in Havahd yahd.

BETHANY. Chance. This isn't a game.

CHANCE. Well how about semaphore then? We could get little
flags and wave from across the room —

VERNA. Ahhhhhhh ... iiiiiii ... it's him!

BETHANY. What?

CHANCE. What?

VERNA. Him. Him! Right there.

BETHANY. Oh my god. She can see you!

CHANCE. What?! Really? Can you see me?

*(He rushes close to her. VERNA turns away, not ready to accept this.)*

VERNA.I'm going insane, that's what it is. I'm losing my mind.
It's this house. This house is crazy making.

BETHANY. *(Taking VERNA's hand, trying to explain.)* Verna.
It's alright. Let me explain.

VERNA. Don't touch me. You're contagious. *(Taking her pulse
from the veins in her own neck.)* I'm coming down with something.
My heart is racing like a jackrabbit. Feel my forehead. Do I have a
fever.

BETHANY. No. It's alright. Trust me. It's Chance. He's really
here. You know that don't you. *(To Chance.)* Say something to her.

CHANCE. Hi mom.

*(VERNA freaks and races away, grabbing the fireplace poker and
defending herself.)*

VERNA. Stay away from me.

CHANCE. Whoa, careful. You could put somebody's eye out
with that.

BETHANY. Verna. Come on now. He's not going to hurt you.
He's my husband.

VERNA. *(But the conviction is gone.)* He can't be.

BETHANY. He is. Verna this is Chance. Chance, this is Verna.
Say something. And be nice.

CHANCE. Hello Verna. I ... I love your hair this way.

VERNA. You're real.

CHANCE. Yup.

VERNA. You're really real. *(She drops the poker and inches
forward, pushing his chest like she's testing the waters. It holds.)*
You're really, really, really, real.

CHANCE. Yes. And that's really, really annoying.

VERNA. I think I'd better sit down.

*(She staggers to the sofa and is just about to sit when — )*

BETHANY. Oop. Look out.

*(BETHANY reaches down and pulls out the vacuum bag of ashes just*

*before VERNA sat on it. VERNA does sit, then takes the bag and
just looks at it for a moment.)*

VERNA. You really are a ghost?
CHANCE. Booo.
VERNA. You're really dead.
CHANCE. Evidently.
VERNA. Are there other ghosts like you?
CHANCE. Not that I know of.
VERNA. Is there a meeting place?
CHANCE. You mean like the moose lodge?
VERNA. Yes.
CHANCE. No.
VERNA. Oh. Can you talk to other ghosts?
CHANCE. No, I —
VERNA. Have you ever tried?
CHANCE. Does this conversation have a purpose?
VERNA. There was so much I wanted to say. Never got the
chance. His name was Harold —
CHANCE. Sorry —
VERNA. It would mean so much.
BETHANY. Come on Chance. Try —
VERNA. Please.
CHANCE. What am I? A.T. & T? I can't do that. Sorry. I don't
relay messages. I don't do party tricks.
VERNA. *(To Bethany.)* I never tried to kill myself to be with
him. But you did. Does that make me a bad wife?
BETHANY. No. Heavens no.
VERNA. In all these years I never once saw his ghost. It never
occurred to me that Harold could've come back to me. I believed in
his death. But I didn't in his spirit.
BETHANY. I'm sure you did.
VERNA. "What fools we mortals be." Shakespeare. Maybe I
didn't love him enough. Do you think if I had loved him more, he
would have come to me.
BETHANY. I don't know.
VERNA. Maybe he didn't want to come back. We were fighting

before he died. The last words I said to him were in anger. Do you think he blames me.

BETHANY. No.

VERNA. There must be some reason. He didn't love me enough to come back.

FLOYD. Maybe he loved you so much he stayed away so you could get on with your life.

*(He comes striding into the room. There's an air about him we haven't seen before. Confidence. He never breaks stride, just walks directly to CHANCE and faces him down.)*

CHANCE. Well, here comes Doctor Novocain.

FLOYD. Don't call me that.

BETHANY. He can see you.

CHANCE. *(Thrown by that. He liked the power of invisibility.)* Oh yeah. You don't seem too surprised.

FLOYD. I'm not. You're not as big as I remember. How you doing Beth? You look beautiful.

BETHANY. Floyd, what are you doing here?

VERNA. He's still in love with you.

CHANCE. Come on Floyd. You're not gonna make this any harder than it already is.

FLOYD. You want to know what hard is? Hard is going through your entire life and regretting every decision you ever made. I'm not gonna look back when I'm sixty and say, damn it, I shoulda fought. Shoulda, coulda, woulda. But didn't. I love you Beth. You are my life's dream. I don't want to lose you. So I'm making my stand right here.

CHANCE. *(Applauding sarcastically.)* Oh great. Really. Nice speech. I didn't see you look at the script once.

BETHANY. Chance.

FLOYD. I want to talk to you Beth. When I'm done, if you don't want me anymore, I'll walk out the door and you'll never see me again. Just hear me out.

CHANCE. You don't have to listen to this —

FLOYD. Close your hole, Casper.

CHANCE. Fine. Take your best shot. What do you want to say?

*(FLOYD hesitates. He hadn't planned that far. He gives a few false starts. Says nothing. He thinks...... CHANCE starts humming.)*

BETHANY. Chance.
CHANCE. Where's he gonna start?
FLOYD. How about with you.

*(He rushes forward and pushes CHANCE in the chest — )*

CHANCE. Hey. What are you doin'?
FLOYD. Sorry. Did I hurt you?
CHANCE. No.
FLOYD. That doesn't hurt? *(Suddenly realizing. Improvising a battle plan as he goes.)* Of course that doesn't hurt. How about this?

*(He does it again.)*

CHANCE. Knock it off.
FLOYD. Why, it doesn't hurt.
CHANCE. Nothing you can do will hurt me.
FLOYD. Cause you can't feel.
CHANCE. That's right.
FLOYD. He's invulnerable. Nothing can hurt him. Without the risk of pain Beth, there's no joy in life. Believe me, I know all about that.
CHANCE. This is stupid. You know I love you Annie. I'd die for you.
FLOYD. But would you live for her?
CHANCE. Oooh, take the cheap shot. I can't compete on that level.
FLOYD. And I can't compete on yours. Annie, if you want somebody to take care of you. Tell you what to think, do and say. Then I'm not the man.
CHANCE. We're not even sure you are *a man.*
FLOYD. And I wouldn't want you anyway. That's not the

woman I fell in love with. I love your independence. Your fire. Your hope for the future. You let him take that away from you, let him live your life and he gets two. You get none.

*(He's getting through to her. CHANCE is getting scared.)*

CHANCE. Annie, don't listen to him.

*(But she is. Actually considering it. Until the door bursts open and ADAM LUCAS is standing there looking ridiculous clutching a gun. It quivers in his trembling hand.)*

ADAM LUCAS. Alright, nobody move. I'm a very nervous man and I don't know what I'm doing.
   CHANCE. What the hell —
   BETHANY. Mister Lucas —
   FLOYD. Beth, he's got a gun.
   ADAM LUCAS. *(Coming into the room, grabbing BETHANY by the arm. Holding the gun on her.)* I've never done anything like this. I don't want to hurt anybody and — *(He sees CHANCE.)* Oh My God. You are real.
   CHANCE. Adam. Don't do this.
   ADAM LUCAS. I can see you.
   VERNA. He seemed like such a nice man.
   ADAM LUCAS. I am a nice man. I just want what's coming to me.
   CHANCE. Give me the gun.
   ADAM LUCAS. I can't. I just spent fifty seven dollars on bullets. I kept buying the wrong kind. What size gun is this?
   CHANCE. Thirty eight.
   ADAM LUCAS. I should've taken it shopping with me. Four different trips to the store. And you can't just buy bullets, or they'll know you're a crook. You have to buy other things with it. Now I'm stuck with forty three boxes of macaroni and cheese. Who's gonna pay for that?
   CHANCE. You'll eat it eventually. That stuff keeps forever.
   ADAM LUCAS. Took me an hour and a half to load it. I'm not

even sure if the safety's off.

*(He waves it madly. Everybody ducks.)*

    CHANCE. Whoa, yes. Jeez, yes. Safety's off. Please don't hurt her.
    ADAM LUCAS. I don't want to hurt anybody. I'm an accountant for god's sake. What am I doing with a gun?
    VERNA. Why is he asking us?
    FLOYD. I think it's rhetorical.
    ADAM LUCAS. I just want the money.
    BETHANY. Chance, what is he talking about?
    ADAM LUCAS. You didn't tell her?
    BETHANY. Tell me what?
    CHANCE. Nothing. There's nothing to tell. You want it. Fine. Take it. Just don't hurt her. It's under the rug.

*(ADAM LUCAS looks to the rug. Smiles. He knew it. Then back to BETHANY. He gestures for her to do it.)*

    ADAM LUCAS. You. You open it. My knees get this arthritis twinge. (So BETHANY opens the floor and pulls out the duffel. ADAM LUCAS takes it and smiles greedily.) Thank you.
    BETHANY. Chance, what is this?
    CHANCE. Nothing. You have what you want. I hope you choke on it. Now take it and get out.

*(His pleasure. ADAM LUCAS heads to the door. Is just about gone when — )*

    VERNA. Wait a minute. I saw a bag just like that in the —
    CHANCE. SHUT UP! (She does. He turns to ADAM LUCAS.) Get outta here.
    FLOYD. In where mother? (VERNA squeaks, nodding toward the closet door.) In the closet?
    CHANCE. NO!

*(FLOYD vanishes through the door, CHANCE on his heels. Half a*

*second later FLOYD comes out with the other bag. The bag CHANCE thinks is real. CHANCE dogs him again, it becomes a game of "keep away"— )*

BETHANY. Chance, what is going on?
CHANCE. Nothing.
FLOYD. What's in the bag.
CHANCE. Nothing.
FLOYD. Let's take a look —
CHANCE. NO! Just give it to me.
BETHANY. Chance —
ADAM LUCAS. *(Pounding his gun like a gavel.)* Excuse me. Excuse me! Does anybody care that I still have a gun?
CHANCE. Give it to me —
ADAM LUCAS. Look at this. People had respect for firearms in my day.
VERNA. Floyd, did you hear what he said? "In my day." See, I'm not the only one.
CHANCE. STOP IT!

*(FLOYD starts to open but CHANCE rushes him. The two grapple. In one quick move CHANCE grabs FLOYD in a headlock, choking off FLOYD's air.)*

BETHANY. Chance. Stop it. Are you crazy!
ADAM LUCAS. *(Digging in his sack and coming up with — )* Wait a minute! Monopoly money! You tried to pull a switch.
BETHANY. Chance. Let him go. Let go! *(CHANCE does. FLOYD stands a moment, trying to gulp air. But he can't. Asthma attack. Big time. He wheezes. Falls to his knees, then topples on top of the bag. Pinning it under him.)* Oh my god. Floyd. Where's your inhaler? Where's your inhaler? *(BETHANY and VERNA are doting over him. They roll him over and VERNA pulls the bag free, tossing it across the room. Out of the way. At the same moment, both CHANCE and ADAM LUCAS move for the bag. But BETHANY lashes out, grabbing CHANCE's arm, stopping him dead.)* Chance help us.

CHANCE. Annie, let go.
BETHANY. Find his inhaler.
CHANCE. Annie.

*(But ADAM LUCAS gets to the bag first. And runs to the door. CHANCE is pulling like crazy trying to get free of BETHANY's grasp -- )*

ADAM LUCAS. Games over. I win. You lose. Bye.

*(He's gone.)*

CHANCE. Damn it Annie. Let go!
BETHANY. For god's sake, do something.
CHANCE. Annie.
BETHANY. Please Chance. He's dying. You gotta find it.
CHANCE. Let me go and I'll look.

*(She does and he runs out the door. The sound of a CAR SQUEAL-ING away. CHANCE in hot pursuit. VERNA is up and searching madly about, trying to find the darn inhaler.)*

VERNA. I can't find it.
BETHANY. Come on Floyd. Don't do this to me. Breathe. Verna?!
VERNA. It's not here.
BETHANY. Floyd come on. What am I supposed to do? *(He's floundering. Then it hits her. She cradles his head in her lap, talking him down like he did so long ago.)* Breathe Floyd. You can do this. I believe in you. Breathe. Come on darlin', we'll do it together. Breathe. Good. Now think of our life together. Concentrate on that. Sailing to Europe. We can do that. Waking up every morning to-gether, for the rest of our lives. *(He's starting to calm. He looks at her — )* Don't you leave me Floyd. Don't you dare. I love you — *(And the world stops. He's calm again. Whole. They just stare a dumbfounded moment as BETHANY realizes for the first time ...)* Oh my god, I do. I love you. *(She hugs him. Hard, smothering embrace.)*

I do, I love you. Oh god, I was so scared.
        FLOYD. Bethany ...
        BETHANY. Yeah?
        FLOYD. ... I ... can't ... breathe ...

*(She releases the bear hug. Explodes into nervous giggles. When they subside ...)*

        BETHANY. I thought I'd lost you.
        FLOYD. Not if I can help it.
        BETHANY. That was too close.

*(She kisses him. Hard. When it breaks he licks his lips.)*

        FLOYD. Do you taste that? You taste like ... wind and rain.

*(They sit for a moment, drinking from each other's eyes. Then CRYS-TAL is standing in the doorway. Again, masking vulnerability with toughness.)*

        CRYSTAL. Alright, I just want to know one thing. What did you mean "You'd miss me?"
        FLOYD. What?
        CRYSTAL. I'm standing here, ready to go. And as I was walking out the door you said you'd miss me. What was that, some kind of threat?
        FLOYD. No.
        CRYSTAL. 'Cause I don't need your pity, you know. So just take it back and I'll get out of here.
        FLOYD. I can't. I meant it. I'll miss you.
        CRYSTAL. I don't want you to.
        BETHANY. I'll miss you too.
        CRYSTAL. Great, that's just great. What am I supposed to do now?
        VERNA. Why are you so angry?
        CRYSTAL. Because for the first time in my life I got my foot caught in the door. I was almost to an airport. I could've gone any-

where in the world when I realized ... ... nobody would care if I was late. Nobody would care if I never showed up at all. There was only one place in the world where I could make a difference. Bethany, you need to know something about your husband.

CHANCE.   *(Coming in.)* He got away. Damn it! That son of a bitch got away! *(Sees them all staring at him.)* What?

CRYSTAL. Did he tell you about the money?

CHANCE. Shut up Crystal.

BETHANY. What money?

CRYSTAL. The real reason he's here. Your husband's been stashing money up here for years —

CHANCE. This is none of your damn business Crystal —

CRYSTAL. Did he ever tell you that?

CHANCE. I was gonna tell ya Annie. Thanks for spoiling the surprise Crystal.

CRYSTAL. You had ten years to tell her. What were you waiting for?

CHANCE. Things came up.

CRYSTAL. It was seven hundred and fifty thousand dollars. That's what was in that bag.

BETHANY. What?

FLOYD. That's what this was about?

CHANCE. Annie. Darlin'. That money was our future. Would let us live the last part of our life in style.

BETHANY. The last part? What about the middle part? How many weeks did I spend alone because you couldn't afford to take me along on your little trips? You were never going to tell me.

CHANCE. I was too. *I was.* As soon as I made a million. That's all I ever wanted, that was my life's dream.

BETHANY. *That's* your life's dream?

CHANCE.  *(Uh-oh. While he tries to pry his foot from his mouth ... )* I didn't mean that —

BETHANY. You didn't come back from the dead to be with me. You came back for the MONEY?

CHANCE. For both. Both. Honest to God. But that money represents my entire life and you let him get away Annie.

BETHANY. All your talk about love and passion was a lie.

CHANCE. No. We can still work it out. You and me, together again. I'll never leave you alone now.

BETHANY. You don't want me. You just need somebody to spend your stupid money.

CRYSTAL. He can't exactly run to the store by himself.

BETHANY. You were using me?

CHANCE. No. No. I love you. I always have.

BETHANY. You didn't love *me*. You loved the idea of having a wife. Somebody to complete your corporate, macho image. I could've been anybody.

CHANCE. No. I love *you* Annie. Everything about you. If love were rednecks, I'd be Texas.

FLOYD. What's her favorite color?

CHANCE. What? This is stupid.

FLOYD. Come on. At least one redneck in Texas must know her favorite color.

CHANCE. I don't know if I can pin down the exact shade —

BETHANY. Let's keep it simple. You don't have to choose from the big sixty four box of crayons with the little sharpener on the back. Just a small box of eight crayons.

CHANCE. Annie.

BETHANY. You must know my favorite color out of eight?

CHANCE. Alright, we're all a little upset —

BETHANY. My favorite color?!

CHANCE. Red!

BETHANY. No, it's —

BETHANY and FLOYD. Blue.

*(Connect. They lock eyes a moment, then BETHANY turns back to CHANCE.)*

BETHANY. You didn't know that about me.

CHANCE. Yes I did. Darlin' I did. I just forgot.

BETHANY. What's my favorite food?

CHANCE. Come on Annie. I don't know. There's a lot of foods. You used to be a little porker. My little piglet.

BETHANY. I always had a favorite. At that restaurant downtown.

CHANCE. Prime rib.

BETHANY. That was yours.

CHANCE. You always had that. I remember —

BETHANY. Only when you ordered for both of us. My favorite musician?

CHANCE. That's enough.

BETHANY. My favorite musician?

CHANCE. The Beatles.

FLOYD. Wrong. It's Glen Miller.

*(He starts to charge forward, but CRYSTAL holds him back with a single look. FLOYD knows to shut-up. It's BETHANY's fight now.)*

BETHANY. My favorite holiday?

CHANCE. Annie, stop it.

BETHANY. My favorite holiday?!

CHANCE. Stop it!

BETHANY. Valentine's Day. It was always Valentine's Day. That was the last time I saw you alive. I begged you not to leave. I begged you not to come up here.

CHANCE. It was the first day of deer hunting season.

BETHANY. It was Valentine's Day! You bastard.

CHANCE. You know the market value on two hundred pounds of fresh venison? That's a hell of a valentine.

BETHANY. Well I never got it. You died. I used to think I'd done something wrong. That if I'd been sexier, or funnier, or a better wife. You wouldn't have left. You wouldn't have died. It was my fault.

VERNA. No. You can't think like that. It'll eat you up.

CHANCE. My love for you is real. A white hot flame —

BETHANY. That's passion. Love isn't a flame. It's an ember. It doesn't burn you, consume you. It protects you. Keeps you warm. *(Looking at FLOYD.)* Love is a very quiet, sturdy thing.

CHANCE. Annie.

BETHANY. What are you doing here Chance?

CHANCE. I'm here because I love you.

BETHANY. What are you doing here Chance?
CHANCE. Trying to help you —
BETHANY. What are you doing here Chance?
CHANCE. I'm scared, alright?

*(The room freezes. That's the hardest thing CHANCE has ever said.)*

BETHANY. What?
CRYSTAL. He's afraid to enter "The Light" because he's afraid it won't lead to heaven.
BETHANY. Chance?
CHANCE. I've done some pretty crappy things in my life Annie. I'm not proud of it. Especially now. Always got exactly what I wanted. I didn't always play by the rules to get it. I cheated and I hurt. Now I'm terrified I'm gonna be judged for the life I led. I've been racking my brains trying to remember if I've ever done just one decent, pure selfless act in my whole life.

*(Beat.)*

FLOYD. Now's your chance.
CHANCE. See, that's what I thought. If we were to stay here forever, maybe I could make it up to you. Give you all the things I didn't the first time around.
FLOYD. You had your chance.
CHANCE. I want another. If you could forgive me, maybe God would forgive me —
FLOYD. That's not the way.
CHANCE. I'm trying to do the right thing here —
BETHANY. Then let me go.
CHANCE. *(Crossing to her, taking her hands in his.)* I do love you Annie. I do. But I'm so scared. *(And he kisses her. Softly. A kiss of love, not passion. And while they hold, slowly that light begins to glow up on the stairs. Gaining strength from the kiss. Growing brighter. Stronger, until it's glorious. CHANCE finally pulls away ...)* Well, here come de judge. Lobster.
BETHANY. What?

CHANCE. Your favorite food is lobster. *(To Floyd.)* Remember that. *(So slowly, in the most courageous move of his life and death, CHANCE crosses the room. With a final look back, he steps into the beam of white radiance. Something in him changes. His posture becomes sure and confident. All fear is instantly drained from him. Replaced with awe and splendor. He takes a few steps up the stairs, enthralled, but he has time for — )* Wait. *(Overwhelmed he turns back to -- )* Crystal. There *is* a tunnel, and a light. Just like you said. If rapture were snow, then heaven is Alaska. And they're all here. Everyone we ever knew. My parents. The kid I gave my milk to in kindergarten. Hey, your name is Bruce, right. Bruce. Mister Johnson. I mowed his lawn when I was eleven. Crystal, it's wonderful. Don't be afraid. We're not alone. Hey ... see ya.

*(And with that he steps into the light. Letting it engulf him. And he's gone. The lights on stage begin to dim as everyone else stands frozen. Now only the "Light" is on. And after a moment, it fades too.)*

### BLACKOUT


### Scene 4

*(In the BLACKNESS we hear BIRDS. Lights come up on a glorious new day. New beginning. Beth comes out, packing up the last of the things. She turns on the radio and MUSIC blasts. Life-giving music.*

*FLOYD comes down looking bright and full of life. They move the sofa, coffee table, and everything else off to the side. But they're dancing. Boogieing to the music, like Fred and Ginger of the U-haul brigade. They unfold a large sheet, dancing, swaying, wrapping themselves up in it and flowing back out. They finally whip it up and let it flutter like a parachute, covering the furniture. Burying it.*

*They bop into the kitchen, just as VERNA comes downstairs. She takes a good look around. Grabs Harold's urn and heads out-side. After a brief moment, we can see her outside the window. She gently opens the vacuum bag and fishes out a fistful off Har-old's ashes. After a silent goodbye, she flings them to the wind. Then another. Then with more gusto than we've ever seen, she is freeing Harold into the forest. He'll rest at peace.*

*She comes back in just as CRYSTAL comes down the stairs, suitcase in tow. She tries to make a clean get-away, but VERNA blocks the door. FLOYD and BETHANY block the kitchen. BETHANY reaches out and hugs her. CRYSTAL stiffens a moment. Then relaxes into the hug. Friends.*

*One last look around the place and they head out. Amazingly VERNA drapes her arm around CRYSTAL and the two of them head out, CRYSTAL dragging that luggage full of cash.*

*Then FLOYD scoops BETHANY new-bride-style and spins madly. She squeals in delight. Then the hiccups start. Harder and heav-ier than ever before. FLOYD carries BETHANY out the door and they kiss ... ... ... )*

*BLACKOUT*

**FINAL CURTAIN**

## COSTUMES

### ACT I - Scene 1

FLOYD:
Black slacks
Blue oxford shirt
V-neck sweater
Herring bone sport coat
Black loafers
Glasses

VERNA:
Khaki slacks
Wine colored dickey
Beige blouse
Tan ankle boots
Cream over coat

CHANCE:
Black jeans
Black turtle neck
Green & black checked
    flannel shirt
Hiking boots

*(Note: Chance remains in
same costume entire show.)*

BETHANY:
Gold slacks
Yellow blouse
Brown boots
Knit Autumn colored jacket

### ACT I - Scene 2

FLOYD:
Black Dockers
Light blue shirt
Burgundy pullover sweater
Tennis shoes

VERNA:
Navy slacks
Pale blue blouse
Vest
Low black pumps

BETHANY:
*For quick change, take off
jacket and replace with:*
Autumn colored ski sweater.

CRYSTAL:
Navy leotard
Blue Batik skirt
Black leggings
Jean vest
Suede fringe jacket
Birkenstocks
Bracelets
Peace sign
John Lennon glasses
Fringe bag

## ACT I - Scene 3

FLOYD:
*Begins scene same as I-2.*
*Mid scene change to :*
Black jeans
Black turtleneck
Red and Black checked
    flannel shirt
Hunting vest
Hiking boots

VERNA:
*Same as I-2*

BETHANY:
*Begins scene same as I-2.*
*Mid scene change to:*
Blue jeans
Blue T-shirt
Cotton plaid over shirt

CRYSTAL:
*Begins scene same as I-2.*
*Without coat.*
*Mid scene change to:*
Green leotard
Gold and red Batik skirt
Black velvet jacket

ADAM LUCAS:
Brown slacks
Peach colored shirt
Cream sweater
Brown corduroy Jacket
Brown oxfords

## ACT II - Scene 1

*All characters same as I-3*

## ACT II - Scene 2

FLOYD:
Black jeans
Light blue shirt
Burgundy pull over sweater
Tennis shoes.

VERNA:
Khaki slacks
Red turtleneck
Burgundy vest
Ankle boots

CRYSTAL:
*Same as I-3 but*
Replace velvet jacket with
    long shaggy sheep skin
    vest.
Carpet bag.

ACT TWO - SCENE 3

FLOYD:
Black jeans
Red chambray shirt
Black oxfords
NO GLASSES!

VERNA:
*Same as II-2.*

BETHANY:
Black floral mid-calf skirt
Cream colored cowl
　　　necked sweater
Low heeled black shoes

CRYSTAL:
*Same as II-2*

ADAM LUCAS:
Brown slacks
Dark brown shirt
Red cap
CPO jacket

**ACT II - Scene 4**

FLOYD:
*Same as II-3*

VERNA:
*Same as II-3*

BETHANY:
*Same as II-3 add*
Gold button down sweater

CRYSTAL:
*Same as II-3*

## PROP LIST

LUGGAGE: Three suitcases and two overnight bags
CREMATION URN
CORDLESS TELEPHONE
EMPTY MOVING BOXES
ASTHMA INHALER
CHEWING GUM *(Lots and lots of chewing gum)*
CIGARETTE BOX, CIGARETTES AND LIGHTER
CRYSTAL'S EXTRA JUMBO PURSE
CIGARS AND LIGHTER
BANANAS
TALCUM POWDER *(Baby powder or flour will do. Enough to mimic dust)*
TWO BAGS OF GROCERIES
BOTTLE OF VODKA
TWO GLASSES
PHOTOGRAPHS
FIRE PLACE POKERS
LEGAL FOLDER FOR IMPORTANT DOCUMENTS
TWO MATCHING DUFFEL BAGS
$750,000.00
MONOPOLY MONEY
DARK SUNGLASSES
ASHES
VACUUM CLEANER
VACUUM BAG FULL OF ASHES
.38 CALIBER GUN
THREE LONG SHEETS TO COVER FURNITURE

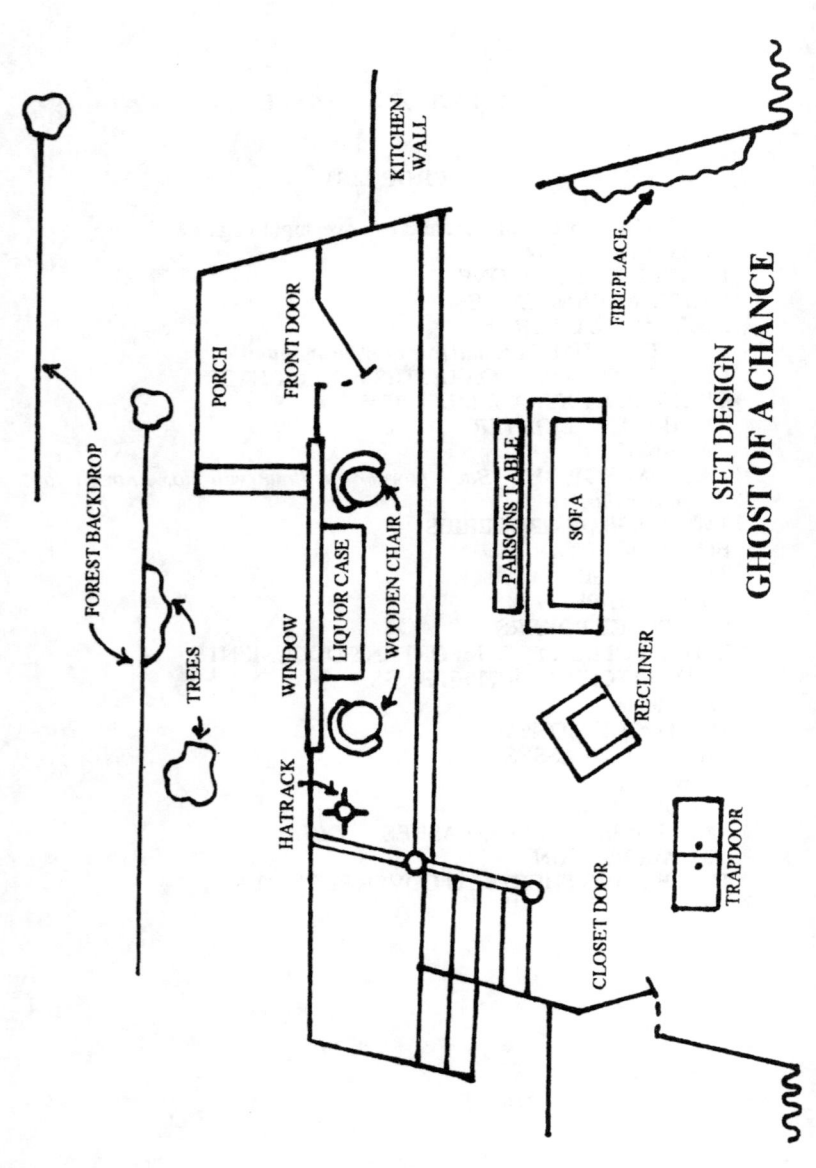

SET DESIGN
GHOST OF A CHANCE

# Also By
# Flip Kobler
### and
# Cindy Marcus

WILD DUST  (Book and Lyrics)

www.ingramcontent.com/pod-product-compliance
Lightning Source LLC
Chambersburg PA
CBHW070632120726
47909CB00004B/1411